PRAISE FOR ANA CASTILLO AND

Peel My Love Like an Onion

"A spicily layered piece of work." —*Chicago Sun-Times*

"Ana Castillo's new novel is a celebration of life lived to the hilt. Sung to the clapping of flamenco *palmas*, it honors freedom and the capacity to survive against all odds. It is a refreshing wedding of spitfire Chicagoan humor to Mexican-American spunk." —Rosario Ferré

"Castillo's prose . . . is as graceful and hypnotic as flamenco." —*Entertainment Weekly*

"The best of Ana Castillo: sassy, satiric, and stunningly lyrical." —Julia Alvarez

"At once satiric and poetic, funny and touching, she makes you laugh out loud and stomp your feet or clap your hands to a Latin beat. She has no need for magic realism, as the reality she describes defies imagination. . . . An extraordinary and uplifting narrative."
—*Richmond Times-Dispatch*

ANA CASTILLO

Peel My Love Like an Onion

Ana Castillo is the author of the novels *The Mixquiahuala Letters, Sapogonia*, and *So Far from God*; the story collection *Loverboys*; the critical study *Massacre of the Dreamers*; and several volumes of poetry. She has received the Before Columbus Foundation's American Book Award, the Carl Sandburg Prize, and the Southwestern Booksellers Award for her work. She lives in Chicago.

Peel
My Love
Like
an Onion

A NOVEL

Ana Castillo

ANCHOR BOOKS

A DIVISION OF RANDOM HOUSE, INC.

NEW YORK

FIRST ANCHOR BOOKS EDITION, SEPTEMBER 2000

Copyright © 1999 by Ana Castillo

All rights reserved under International and Pan-American Copyright
Conventions. Published in the United States by Anchor Books,
a division of Random House, Inc., New York, and simultaneously in
Canada by Random House of Canada Limited, Toronto. Originally
published in hardcover in the United States by Doubleday,
a division of Random House, Inc., New York, in 1999.

Anchor Books and colophon are registered trademarks of Random House, Inc.

The Library of Congress has cataloged the Doubleday edition as follows:
Castillo, Ana.
Peel my love like an onion: a novel / Ana Castillo. —1st ed.
p. cm.
1. Hispanic Americans—Fiction. 2. Chicago (Ill.)—Fiction. I. Title.
PS3553.A8135P44 1999
813'.54—dc21 99-25057
CIP

Anchor ISBN: 0-385-49677-X

Author photograph © Antonio Perez

www.anchorbooks.com

Printed in the United States of America
10 9 8 7 6 5 4 3 2 1

For my mother,
of course,
in memoriam

Acknowledgments

I would like to thank my editor, Gerry Howard, and my agent, Susan Bergholz, for their encouragement and support of this project. My friend and assistant, Elsa Saeta, I can't thank enough for the many ways she has been there for me. Also, I thank Tomás de Utrera. He knows why.

"My life would be a beautiful story come true,
a story I would make up as I went along."
SIMONE DE BEAUVOIR,
Memoirs of a Dutiful Daughter

"Like the French say, God is dead, Marx is dead,
Freud is dead, and I'm not feeling so well myself."
Overheard by Carmen la Coja one day
on a train ride to her *gaje* job.

Peel my love like an onion,
one transparent layer following the next,
a Buddhist infinity of desire.
I breathe your skin
and a vapor of memory arises,
tears my orifices raw
with the many smells of you.
When you leave, Tezcatlipoca,
it is I who have evaporated you perhaps,
horned creature to whom
I have given wings, come back. Rest again, in my
thin arms, limb with limb
like gnarled branches entwined in a sleep
of a thousand years.

The Installments

1

2

3

4

5

8

9

10

Peel My Love Like an Onion

chapter one

I remember him dark. Or sometimes I remember *it* darkly. Yes, he was dark. He still is except that it is not easy to think of him as still existing, and everywhere my gaze turns he isn't there. What's the expression? Water, water everywhere . . . I was full—a vessel, a huge pre-Columbian pot, a copal-burning brassier, a funeral urn, a well, Jill's bucket up and down, a bruja's kettle simmering over the fire.

I was in love once. When you are in love no single metaphor is enough. No metaphor appears just a tad clichéd. You are dizzy with desire. Yes, dizzy, virtual vertigo. Someone catch me, I'm falling in love. Nothing too serious, no ambulance will be necessary. Just a few days of bed rest is needed, I'm sure. With him.

Your very saliva tastes sweet in your own mouth, as a friend once stated, matter-of-fact-like. The science of being in love. She looked around the table, a group of middle-aged women having an evening out. We had all been in love at some time, hadn't we? Surely we knew about saliva and its emotionally triggered alchemy. You know what I mean? When you're in love even tap water tastes sweet. Your own saliva is sweet! she insisted in her Argentine accent. We looked around too, smiling a bit uncomfortably. We looked down at our fancy coffee and desserts. We were thankful when our waiter broke the silence and poured more coffee, dropped those little plastic containers of cream on the table. You know what I mean? Don't you? she asked again.

Maybe that's love in Buenos Aires.

But you must be really in love for the cliché to bounce back like a boomerang smack dab between the eyes with the ring of the gospel truth to your born-again ears.

Nevertheless *it* happens. Love that is riddled with clichés but has never happened to either of you quite that way before, therefore it cannot be a cliché for you. Love that happens abruptly, without warning like a summer shower. (You see what I mean about metaphors?) And yes, it is light and warm and sudden. The rainbow appears afterward on your power walk at the end of a long, stressed-out day, and the city is gray all over and your mother is in the hospital and your best friend's brother is fighting AIDS and you remember the night you slept with him when you were not in love and neither was he, a long time ago.

You put on your new cross-trainers assembled in a foreign land by women and children at slave wages so you try not to think of what you paid for them, and begin to walk the streets of your city at sunset. You say your city the way some Americans say this is their country. You never feel right saying that—*my country*. For some reason looking Mexican means you can't be American. And my cousins tell me, the ones who've gone to Mexico but who were born on this side like me, that over there they're definitely not Mexican. Because you were born on this side pocha is what you're called there, by your unkind relatives and strangers on the street and even waiters in restaurants when they overhear your whispered English and wince at your bad Spanish. Still, you try at least. You try like no one else on earth tries to be in two places at once. Being pocha means you try here and there, this way and that, and still you don't fit. Not here and not there.

But you can say this is my city because Chicago is big and small enough to be your city, to be anybody's city who wants it, anybody at all. Like Nelson Algren said right around the time you were born—*Chicago . . . forever keeps two faces . . . One face for Go-Getters and one for Go-Get-It-Yourselfers. One for the good boy and one for the bad.*

And I loved the good boy and the bad one and sometimes they were one and the same.

.   .   .

Once while I was in the ticket line at the airport in Frankfurt I watched a family for an hour or so that looked like it could have been his but I knew it wasn't. I never saw the man's face, just the heavy mat of Mediterranean hair, his wife, short, a little round around the middle, and their two babies. I tried to see his face to make sure it wasn't him. Not that it could have been him. He didn't have two babies. Does he now?

I was in Germany doing my last gig. Nothing sadder than a washed-up dancer. I was beyond sad. One day you turn thirty-six years old. The sum of your education is a high school diploma. No other skills but to dance as a gimp flamenco dancer, and your polio-inflicted condition is suddenly worsening. Nowhere to go but down, like Bizet must have felt at that age when the debut of his opera flopped and he went home and died of a broken heart.

My mother kept insisting I start cashiering again at someplace like El Burrito Grande. El Burrito Grande had closed down years ago and been replaced by a McDonald's. If she had once gotten up every morning at four-thirty to catch the bus to her job at the factory, my mother said, she couldn't see why I thought I was too good for everyday work. We needed the dryer repaired. She wanted a car. If we got a car, she said she would learn to drive. If I could make my living as a dancer, she could become a bus driver, she said.

But I had spent all my adult life living for the night. I didn't want anything to do with the day. And if this robbery of not only my livelihood but my very sense of being wasn't criminal enough, I had been left like a virgin bride at the altar. Left in a cowardly way, without notice. Left one Sunday without a Mass. My milkless breasts and my love that I had offered and given of so freely discarded like compost to be buried.

Still, I woke and went to bed with Manolo on my mind, except that when I thought of him since he left, his new name was Turd. As I had a bowl of cereal I cursed Turd. I cursed him when I had my afternoon espresso and cognac. Too many years of strong coffee and liquor with Manolío, Agustín, our friends, and bohemian lifestyle as my mother always called it, made some habits hard to break. One of them was loving passionately and another was being loved like the most beautiful woman in the world.

A friend suggested that I see a doctor, as if a doctor could give me a new leg, another spine, make me fifteen years younger. The doctor sent me to a therapist who then advised me to take a ceramics course at City College to channel all that creative fire burning inside me. Six months later I moved to the desert with my savings accumulated from tips, from gigs—at night clubs, community centers, convalescent homes and anywhere our ensemble could descend upon for a few bucks over half of my life—and I lived completely alone for two long years. I tried my hand as a potter and put on the veil. That's what the Spanish Catholic artistas I met there call it when they retreat to do their work. They take a vow of solitude if not silence and become novices. There's a lot of time for reflection while sweeping the tumbleweed and dust off the patio.

When Manolío went away and I stopped dancing I wanted to return to the earth, bathe in it, live inside the planet. But what did I know of the desert or clay? What did I know of the music of silences? I only knew dance, the sound of my heels on the hard wooden platform.

When the second winter of howling winds and sleeping alone was over I returned to the city of my birth. I wasn't cut out for living alone in the desert and came back to my natural urban habitat. I wasn't a potter either, just a dancer who couldn't dance anymore.

.   .   .

On my power walk I discover another espresso café has just sprouted up. It wasn't here yesterday, was it? What was here? Oh yes, a True Value Hardware Store. It appears Amá's neighborhood is really *the* place to live now. Now my neighbors don't have jobs, they have titles. They actually erect white picket fences if not black wrought-iron gates with locks and intercoms. Their change-of-life children's drawings are taped to the front windows. I'm living in a storybook. It's Dick and Jane all over again. See Dick and Jane's house. See Dick and Jane's expensive alarm system. Get off the lawn, Spot.

And when you walk by on your way home, they stare a long time until you're right up to them and they recognize you as a familiar neighborhood face and then they say, Hi. Because that's what neighbors in a great neighborhood do.

There's no doubt about it: this face of mine may very well be related to the one who assembled these bright white cross-trainers somewhere, very foreign, obscurely foreign, like seaweed-and-black-fungus-in-French-Vietnamese-soup foreign, desperately poor and surely-should-be-very-glad-to-have-production-companies-set-up-in-her-backyard-to-give-her-work foreign.

I am just a few yards away from one such neighbor who is out drawing a hopscotch in front of her home with her child. She is really watching me although she's trying to act as if she's not. I prolong the suspense and stop to tie my shoes, which isn't easy with a leg brace. Finally I walk by. She says, Hi.

Nothing gets by you, my jefita has often said to me. My mother has said it before over the years, to note that it disturbs her, my cynical optimism. Nada. She always talks to me in Spanish. It was only about ten years ago that I discovered that my mother spoke English. A friend who had just come back from the voting booths called me. Although my mother is a devout Democrat she was working that day to register Republicans. She needed the money, she said. The factory where she worked had closed down after a big layoff and moved out of the country. My friend said my mother not only spoke English but spoke it quite adequately and wanted to know why I had always insisted that she did not. If you call at my mother's looking for me, she probably won't understand you. Don't leave a message.

I called Amá right away. Why have you always made me think you don't speak English? I asked in Spanish. I have to talk to her in Spanish otherwise she doesn't understand me. Oh, I don't know, she said, somewhat evasively and in Spanish. I suppose I always thought you kids would make fun of me.

Dos: *Sometimes when I get on the train . . .*

Sometimes when I get on the train I lean my head against the window, close my eyes and let myself remember Agustín, who was not dark like Manolo, but cream-colored like vanilla. But not sweet—never sweet. When I remember Agustín I am not so tired. I no longer smell the grease in my hair, or hear the echo of the deafening airport noises, loud pages over the intercom all day long, bla-bla of everybody talking at once, moving moving, beep-beep of those little carts with the flashing yellow light on top carrying people who are going away someplace, career people with business accounts and nice luggage and people who have vacations and take them, and me meanwhile tossing little frozen pizzas into a hot oven from 2 P.M. till 9 eight days a week like the Beatles used to sing and Mexicans still say.

Most of the time I pretend I don't speak English so that I don't have to answer to customers.

On the train ride home, sometimes, not always, I think of

Agustín and his pale gray eyes, sad like a rain cloud, and bushy reddish-blond eyebrows, and I smile myself into a little nap. Six stops until I get off, with long clankety-clank time between them. My feet are always burning from holding me up for seven hours a day; feet that used to dance in heeled shoes, that ached with pleasure from doing what they did so well, feet that, if they never made me a rich woman, at least paid my rent. Feet that Agustín caressed.

Now they are just feet.

I liked Agustín's feet, too, although I rarely saw them. Once or twice he stayed until the morning and I caught a glimpse of them when he came out of the bathroom. Usually it was night and dark in my room or in his room when he took off his shoes. They were very white, waxy-looking, like those figures with the glass eyes that they exhibit in wax museums, smooth, smooth, without blemish or lines anywhere. Never a bunion or callus. How could a man's feet be so flawless? Agustín's wax feet looked like they'd melt in the sun. But I liked them and the tiny blondish-red hairs that grew wild on his toes and at the very top of each foot. There were only a few from what I remember. But it was just a glance or two I ever had of those feet. He didn't know I noticed. So the second time I glimpsed Agustín's feet, I said, ¡Mira tus pies! Because this time I wanted the chance to hold them as he had often held mine after rehearsals in front of everybody. I wanted to marvel at his perfect feet as he marveled over my very imperfect pair.

Why should I look at my feet? he asked. What's wrong with them? He glanced down and noticing nothing out of the ordinary for him went on with his grooming. They're beautiful, I said. He laughed. He laughed and ran his hand in a self-conscious gesture through his thinning hair. Men don't have beautiful feet, he said. Oh, what do you mean? I insisted. Men can have beautiful feet. *You* have them! Estás loca, he said. And that was all we ever said about feet.

Except when he massaged mine, held them tight on his lap when we had done a show and it had gone well and the snifter was filled to the brim with tips and we had all the cognacs and fans and new friends and we managed to get envidia from those who wished for our moment in the spotlight but were sitting in the sidelines, in the dark, getting drunk and whispering mean things about Agustín and me, Agustín would say it didn't matter because they were just jealous and could not ever perform as well as we. Not even in their dreams, he said. Although what we think is life is only a dream, anyway, he would add. When Agustín held my feet in his maestro's hands, hands not as perfect as his feet but far more gifted, I felt that more than money, more than all the champagne in the world, all the silk costumes and pañuelos and brocaded shawls and gold bangles, more than all the lovely things I so rarely got a chance to touch, to own, to try—to feel Agustín's skillful hands, the same that played his guitar in such a way that was not playing but something beyond me to put into mere words, something like fire and a waterfall at the same time, this was . . . But of course if I am going to try to describe it at all it has to be in terms of nature, that is wise at all times, not brujo's magic that sometimes backfires, not skill which anyone can acquire, but fiery orange blazes and thunderstorms all at once. And I am saturated by both. To have those same hands holding my feet and bringing each one up to his lips for a soft kiss, and placing one against his cheek and then the next, oh, I go to sleep on the hot train with the broken air conditioning, remembering that more than anything in the world my feet earned me the greatest happiness the rest of me has ever known.

I was silly with Agustín. I was silly and playful and forgiving. I was everything I wasn't with Manolo. Manolo I did not forgive. Manolo hardly saw me smile and when he had me straddled on his lap, my skirt and slips up, a breast in his mouth, my only impulse was to bite him, his tongue, his lips, his chin, his jaw, his earlobe. I bit his earlobe so hard once he screamed and with a reflexive jerk the chair fell back with me on him. And I was mad and so was he.

When the air conditioning is working on the train I let myself think of Manolo because I cannot think of him in the sweltering heat of city summer. In winter, I think of him all the time. And sometimes I think of Manolo and Agustín, Agustín and Manolo. Agustín el gachupín, Manolo el Negro, mi Manolío, my black Moor.

I wish I were smarter. I wish I knew more things. I wish I could read maps and knew about the world and where Manolo and Agustín went. If I were a navigator of the soul, perhaps I could find them today. But I can't. I don't know anything, my mother tells me. And quite likely she is right. So I make pizzas at the airport now for minimum wage.

And when I feel my body is a huge cinderblock and I have no strength to lift my left leg to take a step in front of me, I close my eyes and try to remember the land they so often talked about together, the village and the city, the blue blue of their sea, the way women prepare mariscos or so they told me and the way that men love men there the way they don't love each other here.

Tres: Who was Manolo?

Who was Manolo? Manolo was soul sustenance for one year.

And to me, Carmen la Coja, one-legged dancing queen who, although I never went to Spain or saw the greats dance at the tablaos, or sing, or play el cajón or the castanets, Manolo was simply the best flamenco dancer in the world.

He came, not like a dream, but when all dreams had vanished. Manolo wore black but his color was red, salted red like mackerel, a salmon heart bleeding deep sea red, though you don't think of red when you think of the sea. The one year I knew Manolo he was a starfish an urchin a dancing sailor happy as Gene Kelly kicking his heels in the air whenever he saw me, but with an underside that was nettle pointed and could make you bleed red from somewhere so buried you thought it wasn't even coming from you but from someone else. But it was, it was you.

I sent Manolo home without a shirt one day. It was dawn actually but in my neighborhood people out at that hour have usually lost something during the night. The shirt smelled of Manolo's dancer's sweat and a little saccharine too from his cheap cologne, the cologne I gave him for Christmas. I never gave a man a present before. My friend Chichi said cologne's always good, minimizes the beast in a man. That's what she said, not me. I put the shirt on over my naked skin toasty brown even in winter and he said, Red is your color. Can I keep it? I said. Then added, I'll give it back soon. I'll wash it for you if you want. I'd never kept anything that belonged to a man either. No, no! he said. Leave it on, I want to remember you lying there in my shirt. I want you to sleep with it and think of me and wear it when you make coffee in the mornings and think of me somewhere, and he laughed a little, thinking of himself somewhere. Manolo laughed a lot but his laugh rang hollow like a big bell that makes a loud-bong warning sound because you've pulled its clapper, not because it's been stirred on its own. Still Manolo laughed and I ran my naturally tanned fingers through his hair and asked again,

Shall I keep it then, Manolo? And he dug his face between my neck and the shirt and said, All I have is yours. Do you want my pants too? And then he laughed again.

Cuatro: I use a butter knife . . .

I use a butter knife to clean the cracks free of crumbs on Amá's stove top. She doesn't think I know how to clean well. This is what my mother says but I do. In our house there are no men. There is only my mother and me and her four television sets, one in each room except the bathroom and my bedroom. With the quadraphonic sound of Amá's TVs in the background while I clean, I remember. I remember everything.

When I was six I was struck with poliomyelitis. Amá did not call the doctor or take me to a hospital right away because she says she could not afford it. My big brother Joseph, whom I have on occasion gotten along with but usually do not, told me years later that they thought I was going to die.

A curandera nearby said it was out of her hands and would be out of the doctor's hands too if they did not get me to a hospital right away. So Amá took me on the bus to the county hospital where services were free.

When I recovered I was fine except for my left leg, which did not work anymore. I wore a brace and used crutches and was sent to a special school for cripples. That's what we were called then. We were cripples, retards, the deaf and dumb. I was president of my graduating class. That was also the year that I decided to become a dancer.

My left foot was and still is like this: bald and featherless, a limp dead heron fallen from its nest. Are herons hatched in trees? I don't know, I only know that my dead heron foot had no hope at all. My left leg was even more pathetic, a dead gnarled limb, thin and crooked.

My right leg was ideal, a fabulous calf that of course worked double time, a slender thigh.

For a long time things that came in pairs held endless fascination for me. Two things identical and equal to each other were the essence of symmetry and the sublime. They balanced the universe and were an absolute om. Two sighted eyes, two ears that heard, a pair of arms or legs that functioned and obeyed one's wishes. One whole brain that kept it all together. For a long time I was with other children who could not walk a straight line.

You could tell one to follow it but he could not see it.

You could tell another but without hearing in one ear he could not stay balanced.

Sometimes a child didn't know what you meant by Walk a straight line please, and he just stared at you.

I understood. I understood everything. But I could not do it. My body went this way while I wanted it to go that way. When I wanted it to do something it did nothing. When I was twelve I took a lot of pain pills. They shoot horses, don't they? I always thought about that movie and about me.

But in eighth grade a new teacher came to our school. She said, Kids, you can do anything you want to do. Don't let anyone tell you different. Carmen? Who is Carmen? Carmen was me. Carmen Santos. My education was being subsidized by the government. Left to my mother, who felt she could not afford a special school for me, I would have stayed home. A nurse at the county hospital told my mother about the school. Mrs. Santos, Carmen is a smart little girl. You really shouldn't keep her at home. How will she be able to support herself when she grows up? She might not ever marry. The school can provide her with a scholarship if it's a question of financial need.

. . .

Carmen, come up to the front of the class, please. That's okay, dear. Take your time. Come on now, don't be shy. We were in a dance therapy class. At that time it was called Physical Rehabilitation Class. It was pretend dance but it was really designed to breathe life into our treasonous bodies.

Her name was Miss Dorotea. Miss Dorotea, I cannot walk without my crutches. Nonsense, nonsense! she said. She laid them carefully to the side and out of my reach. She put on a record of Carlos Montoya, famous flamenco guitarist. We knew that right away because she said, This is the music of Carlos Montoya, famous flamenco guitarist. I had never heard that music before. My ankles began to tickle. The live one and the dead one.

Carmen, do you know that there is a famous opera named after you?

Miss Dorotea lifted my arms. My arms were strong. Here, Carmen, beautiful gypsy girl, put your hands together like this. The students giggled a little but people usually did not laugh at each other in that class because we knew we'd each have our turn.

Miss Dorotea began doing palmas, which she showed us was rhythmic clapping and snap-snapping pitos. Her long neck was poised like that of a flamingo. She had very pretty skin. I was just starting to break out. There was nothing that was redeemable about me, I was certain. I was a sight on the street with a paisley babushka on my head like a Polish farmer's wife and my mother's hand-me-down lady's coat with a ratty white rabbit collar and used crutches.

My hair was always oily and my mother insisted that I did not have to wash it every day. I needed help washing it bent over in the kitchen sink, no bathroom basin, no shower in the claw-footed tub. I was shedding my child's body and I wanted my mother to share her woman's secrets with me, the mysterious treasures in the bathroom that I knew were hers alone, the razor and douche bag and Kotex; things I wanted explained to me and even be allowed to claim, too. I got no instructions with my period, not even a sanitary napkin. Just use toilet paper, she said on my first day as if it would be a waste of product on a thirteen-year-old. With all the blood on the second day, I got some from the nurse at school.

Now this beautiful milky white–skinned lady wanted me to follow her movements, the movements of a well person. Did she want to make fun of us, make us look absurd to each other? Wasn't it bad enough to feel absurd each day when we left the security of our little homes and the people who were used to seeing us?

Carmen . . . Carmen! Do as I say, please. Just try it once, will you?

The music was licking my ankles, the live one and the dead one. I looked at my friend, Alberto, the only other student who also knew Spanish in our class. Alberto was from Puerto Rico. He was biting his nails. He thought I was the brave one of the two of us. If I did not do it, he never would.

Alberto didn't know how to talk. The teachers thought he was deaf and dumb. They'd say it in front of him, Alberto is a deaf and dumb child. But he just couldn't speak or understand English.

I put my hands up the way Miss Dorotea had hers. I focused on the guitar music coming from the record player. I didn't know anything at all about the music or about what she wanted to teach us. I just tried to do what she did so that she'd leave me alone and go pick on someone else. I tried harder at that moment than at anything I had ever tried before. I could not walk right and I was being asked to dance. But I would dance. I would dance for Alberto, little dumb boy from Puerto Rico (who was not dumb at all). Carmen the cripple could dance. Why not? Why not?

Don't look at the others, Carmen. Just concentrate, okay, dear? Do as I do. Miss Dorotea took a swooshing step forward, one long graceful leg crossed widely over the other.

I stood on my good leg and held myself up straight and tall like Miss Dorotea. I wished I had a long dress on like she was wearing that day so that no one could see what I was going to put in front of me next, not a lovely agile limb like hers but a shriveled branch encased in metal. Miss Dorotea had simply willed her left leg in front of the right. My left leg went nowhere at first no matter how many mental signals I sent it. I began my usual negotiations with heaven and prayed a Hail Mary. I promised to go to Mass at 7 A.M. on Sunday. Then finally, maybe it was the early-morning Mass promise or maybe my stubbornness was rewarded, but finally my bad leg moved a few inches. Exasperated I put my hands down and pushed it in front of me. There. It was done. I had done the dance step Miss Dorotea had asked for. I had done it crippled-girl style. What else did she expect? I stared at Miss Dorotea, waiting for her to send me back to the bench and to pick on one of the others who surely would do no better. Instead, she stared at my leg for a long minute. Then she looked around at the rest of the class as if she could not figure out our lack of enthusiasm. No one said a word. No one moved.

Most of the sighted eyes were looking down. No one wanted to be called upon. And then, without turning to me, she smiled and her big earrings jangled and she said with a sigh, putting her hands on her hips and readying herself to dance again, That was wonderful! Well then, Carmen, ready for the next step?

I worked with Miss Dorotea for five years. Because of my intense practice I was able to get rid of the crutches. At the School for the Handicapped, that's exactly what my school was called, her job as physical rehabilitation specialist was just to get some of our limbs moving a bit and to give us confidence about getting around in an environment hostile to our needs. But I took her dance instruction seriously. My mother thought it was a great waste of time, a crippled girl wanting to be a dancer. But she didn't see any harm in it. It keeps her out of trouble, she'd tell relatives. Yes, it was true, my aunts would agree, a teenage girl spelled trouble with a capital T, one said. You can't get them to cook, to learn how to crochet, none of the things we learned as señoritas, my other aunt chimed in, the one with the daughter who later ran away so many times the government put her in a foster home. And this poor creature, she said, motioning with her head toward me as if I wouldn't guess she was talking about me but I saw her from the corner of my eye: ¡Pobrecita! The first guy who pays her any attention at all will have her running off with him!

For my family, studying after school with Miss Dorotea kept me off the streets, from becoming a vagrant, a wayward adolescent, a girl gang leader perhaps, but it never occurred to any of them that I really wanted to be a dancer. Despite my family's lack of confidence in my sincere ambition Miss Dorotea and I worked hard. The most basic step, las sevillanas, which she said everyone in Spain did even on the streets, in discos, was a grueling challenge for me. I know it was really frustrating for my teacher to figure out how to teach me even the simplest steps. Stomp like this, Carmen! PAS-PAS! Her two feet would go. PAS-nothing would go mine. No, like this, again, Carmen! PAS-PAS! And I would lift up my skirt high enough so she'd get the picture. PAS-nothing.

Miss Dorotea would sit down finally, her chin on a fist. Okay, she'd finally say. Let's try it this way, PAS-pas! Can you do that? Stomp softly at least? Don't hurt your leg but at least *act* like you took the step?

Acting is second nature to me. You go out in the world and you act like everyone else. You act like resting, sleeping, sitting, moving, climbing steps, going down, missing the bus, missing your stop, missing a lot of things was just a fluke that one time when everyone was watching you. But really it happens every day, all the time. Yeah, I said. I can *act* like my left side is doing what my right side does. PAS-umph, PAS-umph, PAS-umph. That was easy, I groaned. It still hurt my left side at first, just to pretend. How did I look? I asked. Her eyes sort of went to the top of her head. We can work on it, she said.

And work on it we did, for years. Miss Dorotea was happy that I was really interested in flamenco dance, her life's passion, so she even agreed to meet me after school for private lessons. This meant that I had to miss the free school bus and take public transportation but it was worth it. Even in winter I didn't mind waiting in the cold when it was already dark to get home after I had dance practice with Miss Dorotea. But I don't think she ever thought I would leave the school believing I was going to be a professional dancer.

But I did, so she had no choice but to take me to where I needed to go next. Anyway, she was leaving the country so what did she have to worry about? When I was eighteen and had graduated from the school Miss Dorotea got her big break in the world. She was actually invited to join the dance company that was traveling with Carlos Montoya, whose music by then, of course, I knew well. Before she left she took me to a studio to meet some of her flamenco friends. I really wanted to be a dancer.

That was when I met Agustín. Maybe I looked as young to him as he seemed old to me when we first met, but what he only appeared to notice at first was my clumsy braced leg. Is she a singer? Good! We can always use a good singer in this non-Christian town! he said in Spanish. Agustín was not a Spaniard but he had lived in Spain a long time and had picked up the same likes and prejudices of the Andalusians. I learned later that Agustín meant *non-Christian* not in the fundamentalist way of accusing sinners. Instead, as he explained to me later, it was a throwback term from the Reconquest of Spain five hundred years before. Agustín thought like a Spaniard down to his core although he wasn't. For a gypsy, I also learned later, an adopted homeland is as good as any.

No, no. She doesn't want to sing, Miss Dorotea said in a low and what I felt to be a rather embarrassed tone. Oh, wonderful, I thought. For years all I had ever heard from Miss Dorotea and the other teachers at the School for the Handicapped was how we all had the same right and potential to do anything a *normal* child wanted to do, but the minute one of them stepped outside with us, they were the first to doubt it. No, I do not want to sing! I said to the bushy-red-eyebrowed man who was younger than my father perhaps but who intimidated me more. After I had drawn attention to myself he turned to me. His icy gray eyes glazed me. I was wearing a long dress because I thought of myself full-time as a flamenco dancer and of course because it hid my bad leg. Even when I worked as a cashier at El Burrito Grande, my first full-time job since receiving my high school diploma, I said to myself that I was really a dancer, waiting for my break like Miss Dorotea. I was not una pobre coja as the customers of the restaurant whispered when they noticed my leg and slipped a quarter in the tip jar out of pity for me. I was coja, sure. My bad leg was an unfortunate impediment most times, yes, but it did not keep me from doing what I loved to do and what I was sure I did best, which was dance.

Like they say: it's all in the wrists.

Do you play the guitar then? Agustín asked, starting to move slowly toward me.

I shook my head. I don't know how to play the guitar, I said. I had stopped breaking out by eighteen and I wore my long hair swept back away from my face the way Miss Dorotea wore hers. Agustín was studying me, like a bullfighter sizing up his first bull of the day. He came closer still and continued to scrutinize me up and down as if in disbelief that I did not run from him. He walked around me and then asked, Well, what the hell are you here for then? What is it that you want to learn to do?

I want to dance with your company, I said. From the corner of my eye I saw Miss Dorotea turn away.

Agustín looked at her for a second but seeing she wasn't going to say anything, he stared at me again with an expression that begged me to explain. He did look genuinely confused so I did not resent him. But after an excruciatingly long minute I broke the silence. Why do you keep looking at me that way? I finally said. Am I that ugly to you?

You're not ugly at all, he said, grinning. He turned toward Miss Dorotea but still she wasn't looking our way. No, guapa, you're very pretty. He tweaked my nose, which I hated him for immediately. And who am I to criticize what God in His Heaven has created? he said with a laugh and strutted over to Miss Dorotea. Is this the student from the school for the retarded that you've always told me about?

She's not retarded, Miss Dorotea said softly.

I can see that! Agustín said loudly in Spanish. And she's not ugly either. She's right about that! She's pure gold. I like her a lot!

I haven't met a woman that you don't like, Miss Dorotea muttered. She spoke to Agustín in English. I knew she knew Spanish but I didn't know why she didn't speak it then, as if I would not understand what was going on if she did. She was acting very strangely. I had never seen her act that way before. If she didn't like him why had she taken me to him? I was getting very frustrated but I was afraid to budge. If I did he'd see I wasn't like other dancers. I didn't sway like a palm in the breeze. When I was in a hurry, with or without my crutches, which I did not bring that day, I moved more like a palm in a hurricane. Witnessing that, Agustín might surely laugh Miss Dorotea and me both out of his studio.

You're right about that! Agustín replied to Miss Dorotea. But this one I really like! She can stay! Then he signaled to me. Come over here, guapa, he called. Please, Agustín! Miss Dorotea said. She was dying of shame. But which of us was shaming her? And why? I wondered. Miss Dorotea had been my teacher for five years. She gave me my biggest dream, to do what all the odds said I could not do. Until that afternoon I had really loved her. I felt my cheeks grow warm. And I turned to Miss Dorotea with my best pleading expression to please take me away then and there. But she was staring at the floor.

Fine, I thought. So that's how it's going to be. Oye tú! I called over to a guy tuning up his guitar. He looked up at me and everyone else in the room looked at me too. Can you play something for me? I asked. The guitarist pointed to himself as if to ask, Who, me? I nodded and smiled. And the woman next to him smiled too. He nodded and began a bulería from Cádiz, home of flamenco, and she began to sing in Spanish: *So I won't have to explain . . . that I begin with my lament . . . I talked to myself in the corner . . .*

My hands came together and I began palmas. Miss Dorotea with a surprised expression on her face nevertheless joined me and Agustín, maybe to go along with what he still thought was a joke on him; he began doing pitos, snapping his fingers to the rhythm.

Walk over to him? No, señorito! Slightly I lifted the hem of my dress. Slightly but with definite steps I angled toward him keeping up with the bulería, which demands heavy steps, pounding, pounding. But me, I stepped lightly, lightly, hands raised and wrists agilely turning 'round and about and slowly, slowly I made my way to Agustín. It took forever, but I got there. When I reached him it was Agustín who was blushing. I let out a laugh that I didn't know I had inside me. It wasn't a girl's flirtatious, nervous giggle. It was a woman's laugh. When he put his hand out to me I ignored it and instead spun around to the rhythm of the guitar for a grand finale. The singer changed the bulería: *I gave you a handkerchief and you began to dress in velvet!* And I laughed again that woman's laugh, from way deep down in my abdomen, my gut, my ovaries, from down each thigh and up, up, I laughed and the musicians laughed along with me as we finished our impromptu audition. Agustín didn't laugh. He tried to smile as he swallowed hard, and turned to Miss Dorotea when I didn't take his hand. She's pretty good, he said to her. Watch out, Dori, he laughed. She could get as good as you . . . with a little help from me, of course!

Without looking at Agustín, but still talking to him she said,

Fine. Here you have her. I hope it all works out. She gave him a peck in the air next to each cheek and without saying good-bye to me she was gone. I never saw Miss Dorotea again and except for one postcard from Sevilla that summer I never heard from her again either.

Agustín, on the other hand, from that Saturday afternoon through the next seventeen years, became as essential to my life as the sun that rises each morning to tell us we have not died the night before but just gone to sleep to dream.

chapter two

Uno: The last thing I want to do on
my day off . . .

The last thing I want to do on my day off is to take my mother
to the doctor. We think she's on the verge of a heart attack. Not
today, maybe not tomorrow, but one of these days. Don't get me
wrong. It's not like I'm not going to do it. It's only that she's been
complaining about chest pains for twenty years. Of course, it does
not mean that la jefita was crying wolf, trying to get my father's
attention as I suspected, or that she really isn't having chest pains
now that she's nearly seventy and my father is gone.

He didn't die. She threw him out.

Six years ago Apá took his two suitcases, which my mother had packed for him, the very same ones my parents carried with them on a bus up from El Paso when my two older brothers were small, and he moved downstairs to the basement apartment. My forty-five-year-old brother Abel lives there too. My baby brother Negrito used to stay there sometimes, when he wasn't in jail or in rehab. But Abel now says no. Negrito brings around too many creeps; it's better if he stays away. So who knows where my baby brother stays. As for Joseph, the eldest . . . forget about it. He's Amá's pride and joy but also her heartbreak because he's not only doing better than everybody, he acts like it. His snotty blond wife won't let him come around much. She's not white, she just wishes she were. Amá says who cares about that, what good is she anyway since she can't have children. What good are *they* period, I'd like to ask my mother about her sons but of course I won't. Amá can criticize all she wants, but you, Carmen, she says, have got nothing to say about anybody.

My father called me from work during his lunch break. He could come up and tell me when he gets home from work but he and Amá pretend that he doesn't live just downstairs. I've made an appointment with your amá's heart specialist for Thursday. Are you free to take her?

He knows Thursday is my day off.

What I like to do on my day off is nothing. I stay in bed and read all the newspapers of the past week, including the fat Sunday edition, since I work on Sundays. I'll stay in my flannel nightgown all day, and not until I'm ready to go to sleep at night will I soak in a long, hot bath. Once in a while when my best friend Vicky, who went to the School for the Handicapped with me, is not out of town on business, she takes me out to dinner. Vicky is all business now. A nice car with leather interior, a monogrammed briefcase, a cell phone that ring-rings everywhere, tailor-made pantsuits. The soft loafer type. She hasn't needed a leg brace since the year we met when we were both ten. Why don't you go to college, Carm? she always used to ask me. I don't know, I'd say and finally one day she stopped asking.

Yes, I said to Apá.

She's having chest pains again. She told your brother Joseph, my jefe adds.

My father works everyday come rain or shine. He refuses to retire from his job as a machine operator for a car-parts factory, one of the few factories left in Chicago now that Mexican labor is gotten even cheaper for the same companies right in Mexico. It's hard for Apá to stay at a job where over the years he almost lost an eye and where his fingers are always stuck with steel splinters and where every day it becomes harder to keep up with the quotas that younger workers make with more facility. But he is sixty-four and waiting for retirement, otherwise what good would it all have been in the end, he says.

Anyway, my mother doesn't want rides to the doctor from my father anymore. It used to be a way to get my apá's attention. Throwing him out was an even better one. I'll take the bus, she calls from the other room, overhearing my conversation with the jefito. There's no problem. I have my senior citizen's bus pass. All it costs is a quarter.

My jefito can hear her. I know your amá can't pass up a deal but I don't want her taking buses. Anything can happen to her.

I look over at my mother. She is watching her favorite talk show brought in by satellite from Mexico City. The cure for home-sickness is only a remote control away. Amá is not from Mexico City.

She's never even been there. Still, she feels it is a lot closer to home than Chicago, even though she's lived in this town for over four decades.

They're just about to give out their viewer's recipe of the day. Her notepad is ready in hand. Later, she'll give me the list of things she'll need for it, like cooking wine and costly ingredients for cream sauces, things unheard of in her daily frying which usually contains lard and corn and of course beans. I won't say anything but they'll be on her list the next time I go to the market to do the shopping. She'll never get around to making the recipe. I don't know, she'll say sheepishly when I ask about the dish that never got made and it's been tortillas and chile and beans all week and on Friday orange rice with chicken. Not that I'm complaining. I've never cared that much about food anyway, especially now when I'm smelling stale pizza all day. My mother shakes her head. It looked so good when they were making it on the television, she'll say. But it tires me to think of going through all that trouble.

She's not tired. She's saturated with medication. There are diuretic pills and high blood pressure pills and diabetic pills and heart pills. She really does have something wrong with her heart now.

She confides in Joseph and believes in her firstborn son like Jesus but she doesn't expect him to drive into the city to do her any favors, she says, like taking her to the doctor.

Yes, I'll take her, I say again, but clearly my own heart isn't in it. Six days a week surrounded by at least a million people going through O'Hare Airport, on my day off I want to see no one, not even my mother even though I live with her. Maybe because I live with her. I spend most of the day and evening in my room.

Amá understands. If you are a straight, hardworking person you earn that kind of respect, like the good standing my pizza job has given me lately, like dancing professionally for nearly twenty years never did, or even making a living dancing with a bad leg didn't get me. But if you have a real job, an honest job, you can do anything you want on your day off.

My brother Abel—the one downstairs—is also hardworking and steady. He's self-employed. During the week in good weather he pushes a Mexican-style corn-on-the-cob cart and on Saturdays he runs a newsstand. On his days off he drinks. Buys a bunch of beer, watches some kind of sports game on TV that he's bet on somewhere, falls asleep in the chair. My mother says that's okay, he deserves to relax. But as with my dad, she made him leave too, needled him away if not banished him outright. Amá didn't think being an elotero is any kind of work for someone who speaks English. Abel says corn-on-the-cob pushcarts are the wave of the future for enterprising individuals like himself. The newsstand where he works at isn't what she had in mind either. I expected better things from that son, she said. Oh, leave that boy alone, my father said. But she didn't so my brother went to live downstairs.

What time is her appointment? I ask my apá. I'm really trying hard at my second chance to be a good daughter.

I hope it happens before I die. Before she dies.

It doesn't mean I have to like doing it.

Nine A.M. You can take the car.

That's good, I think to myself, since he knows Amá and I don't have a car.

I said I could go by myself, my amá calls out. I'll catch the bus!

It's okay, Amá, I say. If I don't insist, my father will get angry with me. He won't say anything but I know when he's mad, a frost takes over everything for a long time. The thought of his frosty anger sends chills through me. People think of silence as passive, but as good warriors, tough governments and mediators of high stakes everywhere know, silence is a special method of negotiation.

Despite my father's concern he can't allow himself to miss work. As I see it, poor Mexicans in the United States, including American-born Mexicans, have always had one goal: to work like a bloody burro until they drop dead. The job doesn't matter. The pay is not the first consideration. Work is work. You can never be ashamed of that.

When my jefitos first came up from Texas my apá went out right away to find a job. He came home late that first night and said he had been hired at a construction site to gather old bricks and pile them up. That's what he had done all day. You mean they *paid* you for that? my amá asked in disbelief. Then it was true about the North. There really was work for whoever wanted it. Yeah! my father said, wiping his blackened face with a dirty coat sleeve. Reaching into his pocket he threw fifteen dollars on the kitchen table. See?

My mother could not believe their good fortune. And it wasn't long after that that my jefitos decided to stay in Chicago.

. . .

*U*ntil I spent the last nickel of my savings I didn't want a job. Not a straight job. My dancing paid but that wasn't work. Although Agustín drove me without mercy during rehearsals. Working for yourself is the only way to make a living, Agustín used to say, only a gajo goes to work for other people.

Gajo. He wouldn't have liked for me to tell you what that means although most likely you are one.

Unless you are a woman, then you would be a gaji.

Here we go again, language complicating life for me, as it has from my first day of school. I was born in Chicago but my first language was not English. My first language was Spanish but I am not really Mexican. I guess I am a Chicago-Mexican. But when Agustín became part of my life there was his language too, a language of the ancients deriving from Sanskrit, and his language brought me into a world nobody but nobody from the outside knows about.

The language of thieves, my father calls it whenever I use any of Agustín's words. It's Romany, my mother said once to my surprise. She claims she remembers hearing it in an old Rita Hayworth movie where Hayworth, who was a Hollywood-Mexican, played a gypsy dancer.

Amá, I am not a gypsy dancer, I used to tell her. I dance flamenco.

What are you doing with that gypsy then?

He's not a gypsy.

What is he then?

He's . . . he's . . .

Is he American? I don't like Americans.

You think *you* have problems, Agustín used to tell me about my identity conflicts. At least they count you in the census. At least Mexicans have green cards. Who ever gave a gypsy a green card?

Calorro is what he calls himself. Calorro is what "the people" are. The rest of the populace consists of payos, gajes. It not only means someone who isn't a gypsy, it is equivalent to idiot. For the calorros there are people: themselves. All the rest are idiots.

For a long time being part of Agustín's world protected me from what otherwise defined society as I had known it, getting up to go to a job everyday, working like a fool for someone else, killing yourself to buy things you had no use for, thinking you could really own anything in this life.

Gajo.

Gaji.

That probably means you. And in the end, it meant me, too.

. . .

On Thursday I go to the garage and bring out the family car, which my father has left for the day. I take my mother to the new five-story medical clinic where her heart specialist has his office. After he's run some tests he comes out to see me. He wears a black turban and has a very hooked nose. I like his Italian shoes. I'm staring at his feet mostly because I'm waiting for him to say something first. Ve're running some tests, he says, ven ve get them back ve'll call you. Meanvile, I am prescribing some medication for your mother's angina.

I want to ask what angina is but for some reason I'm having a very hard time saying anything. If I don't ask any questions there will surely be something I needed to find out that my apá will ask me about later.

Polio? the heart doctor asks with a small gesture of his hand toward my leg. I nod.

Vell. Okay then until next time. The doctor sighs and walks off.

I go to the consultation room to help my mother on with her coat. She hands me her medical card so that I can pick up her prescription. Oh, here's my grocery list, she says tearing off a piece of paper from the notepad she uses to write down her TV Mexican recipes. Tamari sauce. Pine nuts. Three pounds of boneless stewing lamb.

Okay, I say. Okay is not hard to say. I don't know why it is so hard for me to say things sometimes. Language is just too compli-cated no matter how many languages you steal.

Dos: On Saturdays I'm forced to make tortillas.

On Saturdays I'm forced to make tortillas. It is the penance of the prodigal daughter, I'm sure. Sons inherit acres and wealth. Women get to make bread, pick up where they left off if they keep a low profile and don't remind anyone of their big adventure.

My mother wakes me up early so that I can do it before I go to work. Meanwhile Amá starts the laundry as she has always done as long as I can remember. When I was a child we didn't have a washer. On Saturdays, her day off, she packed up all our dirty things and put them in a big white sack and into a fold-up cart, went down a flight of stairs and on for half a mile to the nearest clean laundro-mat. During all kinds of weather, just like the mailman, nothing would keep my amá from having my father's clothes ready for work on Monday morning.

When I was a teenager she bought herself a wringer washing machine on credit at Simon's Appliance Store where everything was bueno, bonito y barato as the gajo owner used to claim on late-night Spanish TV. On Saturdays she pulled it up to the kitchen sink to do the wash. During good weather she hung it out to dry on the clothes-line on our back porch. We lived on the second floor and although the building had a yard our landlords did not let us make use of it. We couldn't so much as stand on the lawn for a minute, just pass through quickly on the way to throwing the garbage out in the cans in the alley. You're nice Mexicans, not like other Mexicans, our land-lady would say with a phony smile of old and missing teeth. She distinguished us from the not nice ones I suppose by always praising us for making ourselves as invisible as possible.

Apá, being from El Paso—el Norte—prefers flour tortillas to the corn. Now my mother is adamant again about turning that task over to me, I guess as punishment for not having married and for not having a son for whom I would have to make tortillas one day. La jefita says if I had a man of my own I'd be able to do things right by now, make good tortillas, press pants with a decent crease, and for sure know how to pair socks by rolling them up in neat balls like she does for the men each week.

But if I am not adept in any way or cannot do anything just right, I once had two loves and together there was nothing to add and nothing to take away. Whole and greater than the sum of their parts. For seventeen years I loved, if not a man of my own, then a borrowed one. And for one year I had Manolo and Manolo had me. So what if one day it all went rotten?

Agustín was borrowed but not like a cup of sugar. He would have considered all that belonging to the gajes anyway. A lot of what came naturally to me in being with Agustín, he thought was calorro—the gypsy way. I don't know why you keep insisting that you look Indian, he would say, you are one hundred percent calorra, guapa, not an Aztec princess, but a gypsy queen! The way I dressed, the way I spoke, the way I danced. The way I scooped up the tomato sauce in my plate with a piece of hard bread and drank down my burgundy wine in a single gulp. Not only the way I wore my long hair but the color and texture of it, he said, wrapping his fingers with it like rope. I never knew what he meant by my being a calorra one hundred percent but the idea of being one hundred percent anything appealed to me so I didn't argue.

As a child I had an image of calorras or what most people call gypsy women. They peroxided their hair to a brassy orange, black roots and split ends all over. They sat on crooked kitchen chairs out on the sidewalk in summer heat, wearing low-cut blouses where they had easy access to money stuck in cleavage, and wore high-heeled open-toed, open-back shoes that showed off their longish painted toenails. ¡Sin vergüenzas! is what I heard one of my uncles call them once, women without shame. Their voices were raucous from too many cigarettes as they called out to get passersby to let them read their palms. Come 'ere, honey. Let me tell you your fortune. You wanna know how to make money? You wanna boyfriend? Hey, what's wrong with your leg? You want me to do something about it? Come 'ere. I can help you. Where you going? Hey, gaji, what's wrong with you anyway?

I'd run across their men in the supermarket parking lots. They were always trying to put bonding on any rust spots on your car. They had gold watches to sell. It could even be your watch, before you even knew it was missing. They called you foolish when you refused their offers, real gaje.

Gypsy people used to scare me, I told Agustín the first time we made love. We did it on the broken-down couch in his dance studio, the couch of the thousand and one nights of Agustín, a couch more famous than him. How do you feel about the gypsies now? Do *I* scare you? he asked pulling up his trousers, tucking in the white starched shirt, straightening his collar, slipping on his nice suit jacket. Naw, I said. Why would you? I sat there with my half petticoat on, silk nylons rolled down neatly to my ankles, but still bare on top. I felt a bead of sweat slide down to my neckbone, linger there for a split second, then collapse. Agustín looked at me. You know what scares *me*? he asked. What? I said. What could scare *you*?

You, he said. You scare *me*. And he left without even kissing me good-bye.

Agustín was a calorro born in Cleveland. It may not sound like the kind of exotic place where you'd find a gypsy, but gypsies are everywhere, we just choose not to see them. Or rather, like Agustín always told me, they choose not to be seen. And when he finished college, he'd gone traveling to Europe in search of his ancestors' nomad roots. Going to college was another broken gypsy stereotype. Agustín said everything about his life was different from the rest of his people for the simple reason that his mother had had him in a hospital. Because his birth had been registered his entire life became one payo registration after the next. When he returned to the United States he was no longer August Ristich, a graduate of the University of Wisconsin, son of a car salesman, but Agustín el Bailaor, finest flamenco musician (and sometimes dancer) to ever set foot on North American shores.

Agustín was mine when he was with me but never in the eyes of God, or undebel as Agustín called Him. Nothing short of death could erase the sacred tie between Agustín and his wife—a faraway fairy-tale woman, Sleeping Beauty's stepmother as far as I was concerned.

I asked Agustín once, Do you spell undebel with a capital letter? And he answered me as he always did when I asked him about a word he had just said that I didn't understand: How do I know? He repeated again that "the people" had no use for writing things down because books were part of the payo's world to serve the payo's needs. Whatever the people needed to know they knew. They passed it on from one to the other, century after century, from father to son, from country to country, from continent to continent. Although, he said, gypsies never were too enthusiastic about extensive travel by water.

Why not? I asked before thinking, as usual.

Anytime a gypsy got invited to come to the Americas by ship it was because his alternative was to hang. The officials always figured that he wouldn't make it anyway. And most didn't, Agustín told me.

Agustín and dance and music became sacred to me—a sliver of the life I was a part of only through him and because of him. Every single night, every single hour I spent in Agustín's company for so many years I was enthralled by his strange words, his strange world and his love that was strangest of all.

Then one day it was over, as the expression goes, as quickly as it had begun.

Every summer until then when Agustín went to Spain as he did for months at a time to return to his wife, I waited for letters that never came and I waited for a telephone call that was never placed and finally I only waited for him and when he returned we started up all over again.

At 2 A.M., after our final dance set, drinking our last glass of Carlos Primero that Agustín had brought back with him, hearing him spin his homegrown philosophy on life between drags from his pungent Rex cigarettes, Carmen la Coja clung to the smoke Agustín exhaled, to Agustín's words, to his presence and very essence, oxygen-giving and light-absorbent, like a tiny dewdrop to a pale, wet leaf.

That is how we loved. That is how we survived the sea storms of our calorro love, the love of thieves. That is how we overcame everything, times when we had no work and little cash, times when we had a lot of work and money enough, times when we were apart, his wife's death threats to me and my near-death from her curse, the child we didn't have, all kinds of ups and downs that even a forked-tongue fortune teller couldn't have predicted. We survived everything imaginable for seventeen years, everything but Manolo.

Until Manolo arrived a borrowed love was enough for me. After Manolo, all I wanted, all I want still is the love he brought me—not an absolute love but a love that belonged to me and only me.

Manolo had one year to Agustín's seventeen and that's when I learned that time isn't everything. Time in and of itself does not shape you forever, but incidents, people, a single place can. Something happens and suddenly you look around and you don't recognize anything, not even yourself.

Manolo was spoiled, wasn't satisfied with parts and was all-consuming. With me. With Agustín. They were together all the time. More than either was ever with me. Why does it seem that Manolo clings to you? I asked Agustín. I was jealous of how he seemed to need Agustín as much as he needed to be with me. He's just young, green like an olive branch in spring, Agustín said by way of excusing Manolo's hold on each of us.

I want him to have all of me.

He can't, Agustín said. It's too late.

Tres: For years and years I lived alone,
preciously alone.

For years and years I lived alone, preciously alone. Although my little studio at the Hollywood Hotel was not exactly a page out of *Country Living*. Ambulance sirens shook my old windows at all hours. Shaking caused by the Elevated train going by every thirty minutes rattled my sleep at night. The occasional bloodcurdling scream and the predictable gunshot before sun-up kept me from ever getting any decent rest.

Still it was my very own place. And no one but me ever had a key.

I did get robbed a couple of times but aside from the portable TV and the radio I had nothing a drug addict found sellable. Poverty has its advantages. When you're that poor what would you have that anyone would want?

Except your peace of mind. Your dignity. Your heart.

The important things.

. . .

I'm not going with you, I told Agustín the night that I first laid eyes on Manolo. Agustín was at my place. That evening he was to perform with Manolo's father and Manolío. The great reunion of the authentic Andalusian masters, as Agustín billed it in the newspapers. Even if one of them was originally from Cleveland. I'd be the first to say Agustín was as good as you will ever find anywhere. But maybe not being a real Andalusian was why he never got the credit he deserved. Meanwhile Manolo's father was Serbian, but nobody really talked about that with all that was going on in those countries, gypsies being the first to get the worst of it when conflicts and wars broke out. Although you never hear of what happens to the gypsies in the news, not even on public radio.

You're not feeling well again? he asked. He acted like he was concerned, but he was more nervous than a giddy girl on her first date over his important American debut with Manolo's father. I knew he couldn't care less about me at the moment so I decided to stay home.

A long time as Agustín's star had made me a bit of a prima donna pez in our tiny flamenco fishbowl. It had not escaped me that Agustín was inordinately concerned with the new dancer in the group, a young blond Minnie gaji Mouse from Los Angeles. She had studied in Seville and had a torso as firm as blood sausage and fingers longer than me, who was famous for my hands, so that when her white arms were raised high and her hands twirled in the air they looked like a pair of mating swans.

Courtney. The first time we laid eyes on each other we were as inexorably cast against each other as two pit bulls bred to kill. I'm just glad there were no witnesses. It wasn't one of my proudest moments, just one that made me glad I had grown up with big bully brothers.

For the most part I always got along with women. But in the arena where dancers got up to show each other off, women against women, men against men, usually in the spirit of dance and a good time, there were those individuals who wanted nothing but to reign alone. There was always that one dancer who thought she was better than the rest and had to prove it by putting everyone else down. Courtney was like that. Maybe it was her gringa competitive drive. But flamenco is not Broadway. It is not just a dance. It is how you sleep, eat, dream, think. You don't have to be svelte or even young to be a flamenco dancer. You don't have to have all your teeth or shiny hair. You just have to feel what you are doing, to keep up with the rhythm, to lead and follow your musicians.

I don't think Courtney ever understood that; she just wanted to be the only one who got all the attention. Flamenco was not her life. Agustín had noticed that much. It was a way to be popular. He knew that too. She's always had whatever she wanted, he told me. Her mother started her out in baby beauty pageants, then dance class.

They had a lot of money and only one daughter to spend it on! Like the high school girl who goes after the captain of the football team to make sure she is the center of attention, she went after Agustín and for whatever it was worth, Agustín loved her pursuit.

Until then, until Courtney walked into the studio that day, he may not have been my life, at least not anymore, but he had given me two legs.

Or the illusion of two splendiferous limbs from which I earned my living.

And earning your living is not an illusion.

Courtney came in with a stack of showy costumes over her arms, the rich swish of satin and tulle that is music to a dancer's ear. Four pairs of matching shoes dangling from her fingertips. Her peinetas and fake flowers stuck randomly in her yellow hair, everything at once, I guess to avoid a second trip downstairs to her car. She looked like a one-woman float in an ethnic parade.

Courtney surveyed the studio, checking everything out like Nancy Reagan on her first trip to the White House, hadn't even moved in yet and already planning to redecorate. I was waiting for Agustín dressed in a moth-eaten sweater with two buttons missing. It was my only wool sweater and I always wore it in rehearsals because of poor circulation. She eyed me up and down with her big California blue eyes. I know who you are, she said, but the way she said it sounded like an accusation. Clearly, she'd made me out to be her rival. You'd never have made it in Spain, you know, she said. Is that why *you're* here in Chicago? I said. I was filing my nails and suddenly I had the urge to stick my lucky nail file right up her nose. I call it lucky because it has helped me out of a few tight spots. The impulse to do her bodily harm told me she was already sleeping with

Agustín. No, she said. I'm here because Agustín called me in Seville and told me to come to Chicago. He said the ensemble could really use a good dancer.

Is that all that he wants to use you for? I asked. Courtney took a step toward me, looked at my leg, which I had elevated on a chair in front of me, and then stopped as if to say, Be glad you can't defend yourself.

Sure it was a little more trouble to walk to her than it would have been had she approached me to save me the trip, but when I was finally there I made the journey worth our while. She stood frozen in disbelief that I would dare get that close to her, the file inside her left nostril far enough up to make her think twice about pushing my hand away with any quick moves.

Keep him, I told her, I shit him out a long time ago.

I learned that charming expression from Agustín.

When Agustín showed up later and asked if we had introduced ourselves to each other, Courtney only said, Introductions won't be necessary, thank you.

Whoever heard of a flamenco dancer named Courtney? I asked Agustín, showing a catty side that I didn't even know I had until that period in my life when all women suddenly were younger than me and all of them had Agustín salivating behind them like a dog with no home.

I'm staying home, I said emphatically, although I didn't think he was going to try to persuade me otherwise and he didn't. I had not met Manolo or his father yet. Once Agustín had announced that he'd chosen Courtney to dance with Manolo instead of me, I refused to attend rehearsals.

After the performance there was going to be a party at José's

place, a big shindig in honor of Manolo and his father, two big crows
from Andalusia, the real McCoys. Not phony baloneys like the rest
of us, as Agustín was in the habit of saying lately. Courtney was a
gaji but when it came down to it so was I.

José and his wife were part of our company, but they didn't
seem to be taking things as personally as I was for obvious reasons.
Will you come to José and Rocío's later? Agustín asked. No, I said.
He left in a huff as if he was angry about that, but it was all show.
Such was the state of our love by then, a love dried up like a persim-
mon left in the fruit bowl too long and both of us too lazy to throw it
out.

That night, around eleven or so, when the performance was
long over and I figured the party was just about to get underway, and
feeling a little restless after a loud brawl in the hall right outside my
door, I put on my best black leotard, my brightest long skirt, all my
costume bangles and my favorite earrings (a gift from an ardent
Turkish fan, so it always made Agustín jealous when I wore them)
and went out.

When I got to José and Rocío's apartment I used the back way.
I felt a little guilty that I had not helped Rocío with the cooking after
she'd asked me so I thought I may as well face her in the kitchen
right away and offer my help, late as it was in coming. But the small
apartment was so jammed I had trouble getting in the door. Full to
the brim with gypsies and gypsy groupies, flamenco wannabes and
local artists and who knows what. I didn't see Rocío so I helped
myself to a glass of vino tinto and decided to scout out Agustín.

It seemed impossible to go anywhere through the crowd without a big struggle and I stayed caught between the kitchen and the
living room. I spotted Courtney who I had to admit did look a little

radiant that night, glowing from all the attention around the performance no doubt. She saw me too but turned away quickly. After our first encounter she always treated me as if I were one can short of a six-pack and kept her distance.

Finally I heard Agustín's voice above the other voices, which wasn't unusual since he loved to hear himself talk and everyone else had to hear him too. Right away my eagle eye landed on a face listening intently to someone—who, as far as I could tell, was Agustín. Black, black eyebrows like raven's wings above slanted eyes, a nose much too refined for a man perhaps, a small sensuous mouth, dark skin, not olive-hued but copper. The clean photogenic face of early silent screen star Ramón Novarro, typecast as matador, tango dancer, Arab sheik, in the golden movie years of Hollywood, Mexico, Spain, Buenos Aires, anywhere that such beautiful men were filmed for women to dream about as lovers, as our war heroes, precious sons, shining stars that brought a glimmer of light into our otherwise lusterless lives for the price of a matinee ticket.

He was looking at me too, and when our eyes met he smiled.

I took a sip from my wine and reflexively moved myself out of view. Not that I minded being smiled at by a dark handsome stranger as our eyes met across a crowded room, but just as I was relishing that intense moment, clichéd as it was (and partly because it was so classic), I realized he was *Manolo*. ¡Manolío! Agustín's bailaor boy wonder and son he never had. When I looked again he was gone.

And then Manolo was right in front of me.

Now we were gazing into each other's eyes, eyeball to eyeball, our noses about two and a half centimeters away from each other.

He was still beautiful.

Maybe more so.

You're beautiful, he said to me in Spanish.

Then, before I could blush and say something like, Well, gosh, you are too, or Thank you, and flutter my eyelashes coyly, or Cut the crap, kid, I'm Agustín's woman and I'm on to your kind, he kissed me with a roguish tongue that pushed my lips apart and let itself in just like that.

Afterward he stared right at me again and I said nothing. What could I say? He stayed that close smiling at me until I looked away. Then with brisk motions he made his way to get himself some casalla in the sink where Rocío had dumped bags of ice to keep the bottles of their homemade brew cold, and without even glancing my way again made his way back into the crowd.

I'm dead, I thought. I swallowed hard although my saliva had just evaporated and even the wine didn't get it going again. Then I pulled myself together and left, fleeing like a winged mouse that had just gotten yanked to heaven by its tail.

Cuatro: Everybody likes to think a
girl's first love is innocent.

Everybody likes to think a girl's first love is innocent. That's what my friend Chichi told me that night back in my room. I was so worked up over that kiss with Manolo that I couldn't sleep. One stupid kiss from a young gypsy, a gigolo as far as I could tell, and I knew I was dead. Why do you keep saying that? Chichi said, sounding irritated with me but it was really because she had had a bad night on the streets of Chicago and had decided to call it a day. Chichi didn't have any pimp to answer to since she was mostly muscle beneath the satin miniskirt, garter and bra cut to expose the nipples. She could defend herself pretty well on her own, so she could quit a shift just like that. I learned a lot about being a woman from Chichi, who was a lot of woman for being a man. Chichi bumped into me in the hallway as we were both coming in.

I say it because I am, I said. I am dead. It's the beginning of the end. That boy is my destiny and I am his. And I know already that when Agustín finds out he'll tie us both up and throw us in the Chicago River. No, not Manolo, just me. He'd never do in a man . . . Well, maybe he would . . .

You sure are worked up over this young man, Chichi said. I've never seen you like this.

I just know, Chichi, I said. I felt my face and it was hot. My hands were cold. Yeah, I'm in trouble, I said. He gave me a fever! Can you believe it? That boy gave me a fever!

I started to hiccup.

Chichi shook her head. First loves are always like that, no matter how old or how young you are when it hits you, she said. Let me tell you something. I was thirteen years old when my uncle started fooling around with me and I loved every minute of it. Chichi smiled, pulled off a false eyelash, said Ouch softly, then pulled off the other.

I was thirteen too, I said. When you lost your virginity, honey? Chichi asked. Well, I'll be . . . ! I didn't think you had it in you . . . ! No, I said, when I lost my innocence. I was really crazy for my friend Vicky's older brother, I said. I didn't know if I wanted to tell Chichi my story of lost innocence but I had to tell somebody sometime. Maybe I didn't but I did anyway.

One night when I got to sleep over at their house Vicky said let's get drunk. Her parents were out somewhere. My mother didn't know that or she never would have let me stay over, I said. We polished off Vicky's father's scotch—Vicky, her brother and me—and then she filled the bottle with water, like he'd never find out. Man! That guy was fine, I told Chichi. The father? Chichi asked. No! Vicky's brother! I said. Once we were drunk Vicky said, Whew! It's hot in the house! Let's take our clothes off. Come on Carmen, don't be a prude! She and her brother exchanged a funny look and I knew then that they had planned something all along but it was too late for me to back down. I couldn't go home drunk anyway. Plus it really was hot in the house. Anyway I dug the brother, but I really liked Vicky too only I didn't have a crush on *her*. You know when you're a kid you might have a friend who you think is so cool they can get you to do anything . . . ?

Uh-oh! Chichi said. She got up and went to my little refrigerator to get out a couple of beers. I looked down at her size-eleven pumps, which she had left next to my bed. My bed was also the couch in my one-room home. I think I know where *this* story is going . . . but go ahead if you must! Chichi said.

If you don't want to hear it I won't tell you, I said. I turned around and looked out the window at the Hollywood Hotel neon light that was just about to go out. The sky was turning pink over the fog above the buildings. Dawn is the best time to see what kind of day you are going to have. It was pink and magenta and pale, pale blue. Oh I wanna hear it! Chichi insisted. By all means please go on! I looked down and picked up one of her pumps. God, these are beautiful, I said. Leave my shoes alone, Chichi said.

I really loved Chichi. I just thought she had so much style and class. Chichi once gave me a pair of black leather pants for Christmas. They were the first and only pants I ever owned. I even wore them once.

Next thing I know Vicky and I were making out naked in front of her brother, I said. Actually it was kind of fun even though I was drunk. That was my first kiss, you know? From Vicky, my best friend. She's still my best friend even though she went to Princeton. Did I ever tell you how smart my friend Vicky is? Anyway, nothing really happened that night besides that, I said. I could see the disappointment in Chichi's face and would like to have said more, but I've never been much of a liar. The truth is either what it is or isn't. Like it or not. After we finished our beers without saying anything more Chichi said, Carmen, that is so like you. How could you not think that there was not something a little weird about that even if you never had any previous sexual experience?

How was *I* to know they were both gay? I said. *They* didn't even know they were gay before that! Actually it was by sleeping with *me*—each of them later—that each one decided they were gay! Chichi was looking at me like I was a crazy person or maybe it was so late I was just looking a little crazy. I patted my hair a little. I used to think I turned people gay! I told her. How's that for a special talent?

Are you gay? Chichi asked.

No! Are *you*? I asked.

No! Chichi said, and to show her indignance at my question she went right out the door without even bothering to put on her beautiful shoes.

chapter three

Uno: You'd think I was preparing for a Gold Medal . . .

You'd think I was preparing for a Gold Medal the first years I worked with Agustín. I kept asking him to take me to Spain with him one summer, to see how it was really done since he was always yelling at everybody, those of us who performed with him and his students in the class, which he called a "flamingo dance for yuppies class" behind their back. He said we were all just a bunch of "wannabes." So take me to Cádiz, dammit, I said. If those women are such great dancers let me learn from *them!* Of course he would just change the subject then. Agustín was living a double life and in Cádiz his wife would have fried him alive had he ever dared bring a woman back from America. So Spain remained for me a make-believe place where nothing and no one was real and everything sparkled like a jewel necklace. Even a bowl of black bean soup tasted infinitely better there, he said. And for Agustín's wife, what was America? With all the rumors about him in all likelihood being brought back to her like a deadly virus carried by the wind, probably Dante's Inferno. So she never came here and I never got to go there.

Still, I hung in there until one day Agustín said, I want you to teach these yuppie women in class how to do the Sevillanas. *Me? Teach?* Why not? he said. You learned with Dorotea, one of the best teachers this godforsaken country ever saw and you've been working with me long enough, haven't you? Of course you could teach— even with a bad leg you are better than any of those rhythmless creatures! All they want is to try something exotic anyway! he said. I don't know why they're not just satisfied with going out for Thai food! I'm telling you, I don't think they got this many Thai restaurants in Thailand!

My first day of class on Monday night I was shaking underneath my skirt and shawl. I tied my hair up loosely with a piece of blue yarn and tried to smile and make eye contact with each one as Agustín had told me to. He said, You show them who's in charge if you look them in the eye. I must say I needed to establish that right away, since when I came in and sat down to adjust my brace there was an immediate rustle and buzz in the studio that told me mutiny was at hand. Okay, ladies, I said, clapping sternly as I strode across to the front of the group like I was about to start ballet class at the

Little Princess Dance Studio. Line up with your partner for the Sevillanas and let's go. I turned to Agustín and José, who were going to play for us, and nodded for them to start. The dozen or so women in their assorted costumes and dress also turned and looked at the men, who immediately started to play, so they decided I must be for real and began to follow my movements. Precisely because of my evident drawback each gesture, each step I directed was exact. Agustín was right. They were for the most part rhythmless. Why they were taking flamenco was a total mystery to me since dance was my life. I caught the look of frustration on a couple of them directed at me. Maybe because they were paying whatever they were paying the studio and, even rhythmless, they thought they deserved more than a gimp girl as a dance instructor. Ignore them, Agustín had said. American students always feel that because they are paying your salary you are there to serve them, not that what they are paying for is the privilege to learn.

Don't watch *me!* I finally yelled. I was a nervous wreck. Don't worry about my brace! I shouted, stomping my good foot. Let *me* worry about it! Listen to what I am telling you! *Listen* to the music . . . the guitar is trying to tell you what to do! When you actually know the steps you can tell the guitar! But for now stop worrying about *me!*

¡Olé! Agustín called from his seat, and he and José both laughed a little. I think you're great! one lady called and a few others nodded, smiling. Come on, I said to her, come up and be my partner, will you? She stepped up and stood in front of me. I don't think I got the "paso" right yet, though, she said. Don't worry, you will, I told her and helped her straighten her back by running my fingers over it gently, as if molding a clay statue. If you don't have the posture you may as well go next door and take swing dance, I said. You can hunch over all you like there, but not if you are going to dance flamenco. Now everybody say it once for me, please, I said, as ornery as anyone was ever going to be there. FLA-MEN-CO. If you want to see *flamingos* go to Florida!

Some of those women stuck around in the weeks to come and later others joined up to dance with Carmen la Coja. I actually got to like teaching the "flamingo dance for yuppies class." Usually women signed up because they had just watched a Carlos Saura video with a new boyfriend and thought maybe one night they'd surprise him like Salome with a private performance, or they were off for a vacation in Spain and wanted to be in the groove, thinking flamenco was like doing the merengue, that everybody just naturally got up in a bar and did it. Older women took it as one last shot at being seductive, they said.

Look at me, I told one sad suburban lady whose husband, she said, made a lot of money but he was never home. I cupped her chin and her eyes went left, right, then down. Look at me, I said again. When she did I let go of her chin. Her neck was straight and her head balanced on top like a China vase on a pedestal. You keep that pose when you are on the street, when you go into a restaurant, when your husband comes home. You keep your head up. Dignity is the sexiest thing a woman can learn.

I don't know where I got that advice, plus me a twenty-something-year-old raggedy girl talking to a rich lady like that. But when I said it I shot a look over at Agustín, who had been watching me as always, and he put his own head down and pretended to tune up his guitar.

The word got around about me and we kept the class going for almost six years. Sometimes my one-legged teaching helped encourage those with two left feet while for others it was intimidating because they couldn't believe a woman could dance with one leg until they saw it for themselves.

Dos: I look long and hard . . .

I look long and hard in the magnifying side of my lit-up makeup mirror and one side is definitely younger than the other. As I turn forty I've begun to look like a Picasso forgery.

I hardly wear makeup anymore but I got the mirror from my jefitos for my twenty-fifth birthday. They had just seen me perform professionally for the first time and they really did seem proud of me that year. They wanted to give me something that would help my career, something for a star, my father said. A real beauty, my mother said.

That was also the year that Abel the useless brother finally married after an eight-year engagement. The jefitos thought he'd never leave home. They liked their new daughter-in-law but maybe more than she liked my brother because after a short while they split up and he moved back home. Nobody knows where she went. Joseph, lord of patrimonial right, on the other hand, never worried my parents. He married right out of the Air Force and tucked himself nicely away out in Calumet City where his in-laws live too. As for baby Negrito, all my mother ever did was pray for him. That year, however, Negrito was put in a new kind of detox program and my parents kept saying he's gonna be all right. He's gonna be all right.

I know that there are expensive revolutionary wrinkle-blasting laser techniques being developed, but they only work on white affluent people. So lucky me, who has that "Strange Fruit" Billie Holliday complexion and earns minimum wage, I don't have to worry for now. Anyway, looking older is not my greatest worry. It's my back that's beginning to feel like shattered stone.

.   .   .

As soon as my pizza-making health benefits kicked in I made an appointment with a doctor—a specialist. I really have to get into some kind of exercise routine, I said to her. We were about the same age, it seemed. Her brown hair was getting that faded shade when hair starts going white. I use to be a dancer, you know, I said. I'm sure that helped strengthen the muscles and all these years I haven't had to use crutches

Miss Santos, she said, looking at my new chart and checking to see that she got my name right. She had a little frown, each eyebrow in a sad Z that looked tattooed on, maybe from so many years of studying or maybe from so much worrying about patients like me. It's not the lack of exercise that's the problem here. Although that certainly couldn't hurt you. She put the chart down and sat next to me. Dancer, you said? What kind of dancer?

Flamenco, I replied proudly, knowing that flamenco is a skill and a way of life that's as hard-won as her medical degree surely was. Two accomplished women. Although I must admit I was wishing at that moment that it was me who was the doctor and not me who was about to hear what I thought I was going to hear.

Oh really? She said. Ever go to the Olé Olé Restaurant? They have flamenco shows on Saturday nights. Suddenly we were having a social moment.

No, I said.

Agustín abhorred the thought that we would ever play in a

restaurant and be musical wallpaper. Dance while people ate and talked over our music with no respect for what we were doing, what we were bringing to them. They don't let you take sandwiches and beer into a theater, do they? That's because they want people to pay attention, he'd say. We preferred theaters and auditoriums and nightclubs where they served drinks, to make some money, but not food. Sometimes we even rented the space ourselves.

The doctor sighed and sat down. Miss Santos . . . Is it Miss or Mrs.? Miss, I see. I don't know if you're aware of this but it's come to our attention that as those people who had polio as children get older, in some cases the polio returns.

I blinked.

It's too early to tell yet if this is the case with you. We'll have to do the tests to see what we can find out. There's really no way of knowing for sure.

There is no way of telling except that these past nights I've been waking up to my leg going numb and the whole following day I can barely use it at all. But as Amá always says in Spanish, To eat one must work! So I get up anyway and make it through another day. But who can know if I'll be a cripple like when I was six years old and had to learn to walk again, except that now the other leg hurts too, and for the first time in twenty years I must order a new pair of crutches.

Tres: That year when I was twenty-five . . .

That year when I was twenty-five I didn't use my crutches at all and even did without the brace for a while. People really didn't know about my leg until they saw me walk. When I danced I told myself that they could not tell. I always did solos or danced with Agustín where alone or with him I had a chance to dance my own way. I wouldn't be able to keep up with the other women, because in such a number the object was to show each other up. You could have told that right away I was the deer with a broken hoof.

Still, I was happy. And it seemed that year that my jefitos had managed to solder something together of their marriage and they were also happy. For my birthday they gave me the mirror that they had gone all out for and picked up at Sears. Brand-new and professional looking. It wasn't cheap either, my father said. He's always had that habit, a carryover from his dirt-poor upbringing, I suppose, of telling you how much he paid for something, even gifts. They really were trying. For once, they were proud of themselves, proud of their new bungalow-style mortgaged home, proud of their new refrigerator with automatic ice-maker and proud of their children, before everything began to unravel like one of my amá's acrylic afghans that's been put in the washing machine too many times.

A few years after our family fell into need of repair, maybe to make up for the disappointing children, my father bought my mother a dog for their anniversary. Actually he got it from a guy at work who was giving away some puppies. It was a chihuahua named Macho. Macho is still alive but he has arthritis now. Macho the arthritic chihuahua, my parents' only grandchild.

In Mexico they say that chihuahuas are good to have around children with asthma. A chihuahua helps cure asthma, my mother told me once. Great, I said.

I can't say for sure what the bomb was that finally exploded my jefitos' marriage because my amá doesn't tell me things. All I know is that one day I came by to visit and my mother announced to no one in particular, just said it aloud, that Apá had gone downstairs to live with my brother. I was there to get a bite of Amá's homemade tortillas and beans, and since I was really hungry and broke that day I didn't push the issue because she might tell me to get out too. I decided it was best for me not to pursue it.

I think it's the woman shop steward at Apá's job that Amá's worried about, my brother Joseph said one day after my father had settled in downstairs. My mother likes to confide in her oldest son. Because he's so conservative she thinks his opinion can be relied on. What makes you say that? I asked Joseph. I knew what made him say that was that Amá had confessed as much. I don't know, he said, shrugging his shoulders, like he didn't want to betray his mother's trust. He just comes home talkin' about that girl all the time, he said. She's a vegetarian. Did you know that?

I stared at Joseph. How could a man who had left Texas as a preschooler be so darn tejano, with his monogrammed buckled belts, Western boots, and that annoying way of always acting like he was pulling up his pants when he was about to announce something. What d'you mean? I asked. That being vegetarian means you're a husband stealer?

Well, he said. Who does she think she is?

By not eating meat? I asked, still in disbelief at my older brother's reasoning. Well then, cattle-rustler, let's lynch her, why don't we!

Joseph shook his head. You know what's wrong with you, Carmen? You need a man.

I got a man! I said, the blood rushing to my head. I got a lot of men!

That's the problem, he said calmly. You ain't got one to take care of you, to tell you what's what and to keep you in line.

Joseph is my least favorite brother.

Since I really want to be a good daughter, I don't ask questions. To be a good daughter you just accept the acts of your parents, however ludicrous you might think them; the critical comments, however unsolicited and insensitive; the demands, however maddening; and the emphatic declarations, however contradictory. You do everything in your power to fulfill their wishes, however senseless they sound, and you never ever question a parent. It is the duty of the good daughter to provide her parents with a home if they need it. Look after their needs and desires. Never protest. Don't complain. Just eat the tortillas and run.

Cuatro: When I found out that I was
pregnant it was both the worst and . . .

When I found out that I was pregnant it was both the worst and happiest time I remember. It was also the year I was twenty-five. My mother yelled at me for a week before she sent me off to live with the scoundrel who had gotten me that way. But Agustín was not around. As soon as I told him the news he went back to Spain. I'm sure now that he was afraid the word would get back to his wife quickly and he wanted to get to her beforehand.

I rented a studio on Wilson Avenue. It was one of those hotel-apartment places that were really cheap rooms for people like me with nowhere else to go. I ended up making that room on the seventh floor of the Hollywood Hotel, with cracked plaster, roaches and all, my home for nearly a dozen years until it was torn down in order to build a big, sparkling new, fully equipped gym, one of those health clubs that require memberships. Sure, I think, it's exactly what the displaced residents of the Hollywood Hotel—the poor whites, Winnebagos from Wisconsin, the new Salvadoran immigrants, the drunks, drug addicts, streetwalkers and those one-step-away-from-homelessness—need, to buff out.

For a whole year Agustín had talked about how much he wanted us to have a baby together. Inmaculada, his wife, was unable to conceive, he said, and he wanted a child more than anything in life. I thought he'd be ecstatic when I gave him the news. So when my amá said that I'd better get married or get out of her home, I moved out. I figured Agustín would stand by me. I knew we couldn't get married, but that didn't matter to me.

I did not expect him to book the first flight out. He gave me some kind of pitiful excuse about having to go for business reasons, but I knew what was up.

Don't expect him to come back, Rocío, the group's singer, told me. She and the rest were really angry with me. What are we going to do without a manager? she asked. As if I had any answers. It didn't look like he'd come back, not on his own, so I did the only logical thing that occurred to me, I went to see a palm reader.

I passed Hermana Ana's hand-painted sign every day but I just couldn't get myself to let go of five dollars that I could eat with to find out about my future. But when Agustín took flight as quick as a reflex, like a duck who goes south for the winter without a debate, just does it instinctively for the sake of survival of the species, I was ready to pay anything to know something.

Your jealousy drove him away, she told me. She'd asked for five dollars up front. No guarantees, understand? I didn't like her. Still, I gave her the five dollars.

I was never jealous, I lied.

Well then, someone else is jealous. You'd better be careful. She can do you harm.

I knew the fortune teller was right because Agustín told me that he himself was afraid of his wife's powers over him. How was I going to protect myself and my baby from Inmaculada's curse?

I'll give you something to wear around your neck to protect you. It's gonna cost you, so I hope you can afford it, she said, sizing up my used clothes. They weren't in bad condition because I had an eye for quality and luck finding true vintage, but of course nothing I wore looked first-time. Meanwhile, if you really want to take care of this woman who's taken your man from you, you got to send her evil right back to her.

Okay, I said.

That'll cost you twenty dollars, she said.

I didn't have twenty on me, but I went back to the Hollywood Hotel where I hid my savings underneath a broken tile in the bathroom and I came back with it the same day.

She gave me a little pouch of purple cloth no wider than a man's thumb and half the size all sewn up so that I couldn't see what was inside. Tie that to a rope or chain or something, she instructed, and wear it around your neck until he comes back. Don't take it off, not even when you take a bath. Watch how you wear it. You don't want to choke at night, she added.

What about . . . ? I started to ask.

What about reversing the evil? she asked, getting up and readying herself for the next customer. Don't worry about that, honey. I've already taken care of it.

In the meantime, I registered at the health clinic down the

street from me for a prenatal exam. They charged a scale rate and because I had no real source of income everything was free. Me and my baby were okay, they said.

I went to the Salvation Army store, also in my neighborhood, and whenever I saw anything that I thought the baby would need I'd pick it up—soft, clean, although worn and faded blankets, a little plate-and-spoon set stenciled with the Three Little Pigs. My favorite find was a copy of *The Little Engine That Could*. The kids I grew up with and I didn't get bedtime stories read to us. After reading it for the first time at the Salvation Army store I read it over and over, The Little Engine That Could that saved the day for all the little children.

Of course our group was out of work because Agustín had left so abruptly. My savings were beginning to dwindle quickly, so I ate only once a day. I stopped buying things that cheered me up at the Salvation Army store. Because at the Hollywood Hotel each room was charged for use of electricity I didn't watch TV at all. Sometime back my father had lent me his emergency lantern that he kept in the trunk of his car so I didn't use any lights either. I listened to my transistor radio until the batteries ran down.

I hate to say it but one thing I did not stop doing was drink.

How much harm could a glass of brandy at night to help me sleep and keep me warm between thin sheets and one blanket do? I reasoned. Or a glass of wine that livened up a dinner of canned soup? But it wasn't just a glass of brandy at night or a glass of wine a day. Whenever I had a visit from a friend or went to visit a neighbor staying at the Hollywood Hotel, all it was was liquor and cigarettes to pass the day and night.

Meanwhile, as the weeks went by I wondered if the fortune teller's magic was working for me.

Until one night I woke up to a wet feeling between my legs. I turned on the light half asleep thinking I may have peed in my sleep. Being pregnant was making my body do weird things all the time. But instead it was blood, bright red and oozing, and the bottom half of my nightgown was already sopped.

My telephone was disconnected but there was a pay phone downstairs just outside the entrance. I padded my panties with nearly a roll of toilet paper and put on my coat. Downstairs I called an ambulance and waited outside until they came.

Who called an ambulance? the paramedic who jumped out of the vehicle first asked me after I signaled them down like a taxi. I did, I said.

What's wrong? he asked. Another guy carrying a medical bag had come out, too. I opened my coat.

Have you been shot? the first guy asked.

No, I said. I'm hemorrhaging.

Jeez, the other guy said. Let's get her in.

A week after I got home from the hospital, my womb empty and scraped like a carefully carved-out melon, Agustín returned. You don't know what I've been through, were his first words when he came into my home.

You? I said.

I'd lain in bed the whole week. Sometimes if Chichi went out for dinner with some trick she'd bring back Chinese leftovers or pizza. She'd leave a beer or a half bottle of cheap wine for me too. Chichi meant well but you can't expect a whole grain diet from someone who makes her living on the street.

One day I got up and put all the baby things in the closet because I couldn't bear to look at them. That night I got up again and threw them all out of the window. The next morning they were all gone except for one newborn blanket below that got stuck on the fence and was too high to reach from the ground. It just waved and waved in the breeze.

Even though my home was tiny, the few furnishings run down and, if the truth be known, the whole place downright dreary, I had fixed it up my own way. I liked to collect pretty things, treasures found mostly in the secondhand stores and flea markets I liked to browse through on my days off. Cracked Hummel porcelain figures, a clay replica of a pre-Columbian goddess with part of the head chipped off, a unicorn without a horn made of hand-blown glass like the kind Tennessee Williams wrote about in his play. I collected presidents' plates and china cups, Danish crystal candy dishes. Many were chipped and mismatched or the only one of its kind so I know they weren't worth much, but they were very pretty to look at.

Pretty to look at, lovely to hold, but if you break it, consider it sold. Chichi used to like to say that. She was talking about herself. Years later, just before Chichi was able to have the operation that would have made her a total woman, having worked and saved years for it, I heard that someone found her pre-op corpse in a hallway, broken forever. Nobody claimed the body and it went to the city morgue.

I still miss Chichi.

Most of what I had collected was shattered and lay on the floor when Agustín showed up. Obviously it was left there for his sake.

What happened here? he asked.

So you noticed?

What do you mean? What are you talking about? He got the broom and began to sweep some of it away as if I had just let the place get dusty, although he didn't pick any of it up. He reeked of guilt but I knew he wouldn't own up to it. Accusing him of anything at that moment would have only gotten his hypocritical indignation.

So what happened to *you?* I said calmly. As if it had been a picnic for me. I lay wearing the same nightgown I had gone to the hospital in, unwashed. There were a couple of dirty glasses and bowls next to the bed. Dishes in the sink. Agustín kept looking around. He seemed a little spooked and resentful of my pathetic state. You'd think I was acting out some deserted woman scene instead of actually having lived it.

Inmaculada was really sick. That's why I had to go, he said. He always referred to his wife by name as if I knew her. I couldn't tell you because, you know. But that's why I had to leave so quickly.

When I didn't say anything, he continued. She got better. But for a while, we all thought we were going to lose her.

Well, I'm so glad that you didn't, I said.

I pushed the blanket off and noticed that Agustín winced when he saw the stained nightgown but he said nothing. He sat down at the table and stared at me. Say something, querida. Please, he said.

Welcome back.

Of course I didn't mean it and for three months I didn't speak to Agustín. Rocío came by and convinced me to return to the company for the group's sake if not Agustín's, and for my sake, since I was out of cash and two months behind the rent by then. So I did.

. . .

During that whole year after my mother sent me out of her house I did not see my family. Except once, after Apá found out that I was living not far from them, he came by to see me. It was obvious that I wasn't pregnant anymore but he didn't ask about it. My father's always had a hard time talking about anything personal. He asked if I was all right and when I assured him that I was, he left without finishing the cup of coffee I'd insisted he have with me. Too strong, he said. He did not leave any money, although I looked around, under things like the napkin, just in case. He did not invite me over. To eat or otherwise. Well, we were just worried about you, that's all, he said. Saying *I* would have been too personal for my jefito, although I knew he was really speaking mostly for himself since there was nothing stopping my mother from coming with him, nothing at all but stubbornness I figured. There was nothing preventing my brothers or their wives from coming to see me either, except that of course I guess they had problems of their own. As for Negrito—he *is* a problem. My baby brother is tender, smart, a good artist, but he might also rob you blind. So it goes without saying that nobody in my family would tell him how to find me.

I never got pregnant again, although Agustín and I still remained lovers for a decade after that. I used birth control. And when the whole AIDS thing became something that even someone like me with a longtime sometime partner should be concerned about, I made Agustín do something that seemed to go against his entire sense of being, everything he stood for, unheard of in his philosophical repertoire (recited to me often) about what it was to be a man. Use rubbers or you can go back to your wife, I said. As you can guess, if it's hard to get most men to use one—men-men, men who are men and therefore don't wear rubbers—it was nearly impossible in the case of Agustín where there isn't even a word for rubber in his language.

·   ·   ·

*T*en more years with Agustín and I was feeling pretty old, older than him, older than I feel now. Funny how a man can do that to a woman. But it wasn't me who was old. I felt bad from a *love* gone stale. Worse, it was a love that was never mine and had never been mine. It was never going to be won. Agustín's wife had won the battle of the curses and she had won the war over Agustín's love as far as I was concerned.

She might be able to live with having a husband who was clearly not faithful to her, who didn't even stay with her half the time, but that wasn't good enough for me. It might be okay for her, I told Agustín the last time I let him touch me. But it's not enough for me.

What's bothering you, mi amor? He said "my love" out of habit, without real desire, and that bothered me too. Everything bothered me about Agustín suddenly, suffocated me like I was nailed alive inside a coffin. How much his cigarettes stank up my little home, the way his nose lit up like the Statue of Liberty's torch from so much drinking, how he exaggerated all his stories.

You. You're bothering me, I said. I didn't mean just at that moment as his hand had reached over to my breast in the dark and I pushed it away. I meant his whole presence in my life was suddenly nothing more than an annoyance.

God, as much as I hated to think of my parents still being intimate, of ever being intimate, I suspected then and there exactly what must've driven Amá to send my father away, not just out of the bed but even out of her home. That callused, clammy, worn-out, brusque hand of a man that reaches out of habit and horniness for your tired breast in the dark.

Bien, he said, thinking my spurning would pass like a bad

headache the next day. He turned over and two seconds later he was snoring as if he didn't have a care in the world.

Cinco: Aren't you Carmen la Coja?

Aren't you Carmen la Coja? this guy asked me once in a bar. It was actually more than a bar, it was the first and only Sapogón restaurant in town. They served what appeared to my biased taste to be impostor Mexican food. But actually it was Sapogón cuisine. In the 1980s all kinds of people were moving to Chicago from south of the border, variations of the Mexicans and Puerto Ricans I was used to when I was growing up. There were people from countries I'd never heard of, Sapogonia being one of them. South of Mexico and not an island is all I knew about it when Agustín said, We're invited to a private party to celebrate Sapogonia Independence. Lots of food, wine. It's gonna be a lot of fun.

Do I have to dance? Is the catch that we have to perform? I wondered. Come on now, Agustín said. Don't you think I would tell you?

For once he was totally sincere about our going out together to simply enjoy ourselves, and between the cheap pink bubbly wine that our host was serving freely and the platters of roasted pork with imported cooked vegetables that were passed around, everyone— Sapogonian or not—was in an overly satiated mood. A Roman fest made up of political refugees. It wasn't just Sapogonians who were there, but like I said, all kinds of Spanish-speaking people now making Chicago their home. The heartsick Cubans sang "Guantan-amera" and the lonely Mexicans sang "Cielito Lindo" and the Colombians sang old cumbias and then the Peruvians sang a potpourri of polkas and the Argentines capped it all off with one tango after the next. Just about then someone with a guitar leaned over and whispered: Aren't you Carmen la Coja? I smiled at him. I'm Máximo Madrigal, he said, smiling back, and kissed my hand. He was wearing gaucho pants although he wasn't a gaucho. Quite an outfit to pull off outside of the pampas but he came on right away as the type who could pull off just about anything. I wasn't doing too bad myself in a long ruffled skirt and low-cut bodysuit. I didn't really have going-out clothes so I wore my costume.

How did you know? I asked in Spanish and did not blush from his direct gaze. So many years with Agustín, immersed in the calorro lifestyle, had worn out all the blushes I ever had.

You are famous all over town, Max said, smiling and signaling with his guitar that he would play for me if I would dance. You can't refuse me, he said. It's my country's birthday. Go ahead, said Agustín from way over at the bar. He had antelope ears and could hear anything said to me even from across a loud room. I could tell he didn't like Máximo one bit. So long together and Agustín was still jealous of anyone who took a second look at me. So I got up.

Máximo followed me with his guitar and Agustín followed Max. People moved aside seeing me getting ready to dance and some started to applaud already and a few whistled. In all that time of dancing throughout the city it was only that night that I realized I was indeed famous all over town. A table was stripped of its table-cloth and placed in the center of the room. Two guys lifted me up so gracefully it looked as if we had practiced that move all day. Max started playing an alegría when I heard Agustín say, That's not how it goes. Play whatever you want, I said to Máximo and I began to snap my fingers to the rhythm and lifted my hands up to start my dance. The secret to my one-legged flamenco style was to take my time. I took a few steps, all the while watching Max. I found him handsome and charming in a caddish kind of way in his absurd Robin Hood shirt and patent-leather boots. Even though at that point I still loved Agustín you could hear me tearing away from him if you listened very carefully, like when you sit down and your matador-tight capris split up the rear seam. Agustín looked around to see if anybody else had heard it too and backed away. Max laughed and handed Agustín his guitar when someone said, Rumba! And someone else said, Tango! Let's all merengue! some bubblied-out Dominican shouted from a table in the back where it looked like he couldn't even get up. It made me laugh so hard I took off my flowered shawl and threw it down around Max's shoulders like a net. Yeah! Dance with me! I said to him. Max brought me back down. Thankfully I did not have the brace on that night and my heels touched the floor with a soft one-two step since one leg is shorter than the other.

I don't know how to tango, I don't think . . . I confessed in Max's ear. He was already holding me so tight my breasts were squash blossoms against his chest. Yes you do, he said. Let's show them. As if on cue someone was at the piano singing *El día que me quieras* . . . The day you love me . . . as unforgettable a tango as you'll ever want to hear. Max put his hand firmly against my lower back, looked hard into my eyes and said, *Just follow me*. And we began to move like Al Pacino did in that movie of his. In fact when I saw it years later I remembered how I, not blind (like you need eyes to dance anyway) but with one crazy leg with a mind of its own, danced tango for the first time that night. Max and I tangoed not just across the room, everybody moving out of our way, but out of the door, which someone had opened for us as a joke as Max led me out cheek-to-cheek and *poof!* Like a Houdini magic trick, we were both gone.

Seis: Finally we met.

Finally we met. Manolo and I. Agustín introduced us formally at rehearsal on the Tuesday after our first flash encounter. Agustín did not say, This is my woman, as he used to, only, This is Carmen, and Manolo and his father sized me up like the prize cow at the county fair and smiled but said nothing. Manolo acted as though we had never seen each other before.

You missed a great performance, Agustín told me.

Perhaps, I said. Manolo smiled, brushed off a little lint from his lapel and looked away.

Perhaps? Agustín asked, obviously not privy to my joke but immediately put on alert because, Agustín being Agustín, he could sense deceit from around the corner. Double-crossed and double-dealing, "gyp" as in gypsy. It may be an unfair stereotype but the Rom people, as Agustín said so many times, have been sold out by everyone long enough to have developed a watch-guard gene in their immune system.

In my own case I'm not sure why duplicity came so easily to me that afternoon. I could still feel that cur's kiss from Saturday night on my teeth and I rubbed them, a little self-conscious that with a closer look Agustín would detect its traces like a nicotine stain. Nevertheless when love is new surrendering one's conscience seems to be par for the course.

You think it's your soul, but it's not, it's your conscience.

So it was that the three of us, righteous lovers of love and life (if not always loving each other right), began our ever-resplendent braid of deceit and desire. Each taking his turn slowly, with great finesse until we'd reached that inevitable fallow end oh-such-a-brief-time later.

My compai here gave the performance of a lifetime! Agustín added, but he was talking about the old man while he was looking at Manolo, scrutinizing him for a clue although to what he wasn't yet sure.

I'm sorry, I apologized to the compai. Don't worry, he said. There will be plenty more. Manolo's father, whom Manolo called Bato in caló, was dying of stomach cancer. He had started chemo-therapy so he wore a Bing Crosby Palm Springs–looking hat to con-ceal his balding head. Most people don't like talking about death but the Rom really don't like it. Death talk is so taboo just uttering the word could get you banished from the tribe. So no one brought up the bato's illness.

Manolo, in the customary mourning black of the flamenco dancer, was wearing short suede boots with the high dancer's heels. His hair was impeccably sculptured, a glistening cascade of tight curls, shorter on the top and around the ears, long in the back.

He looked so good he made my arms itch.

We were all a little too aware of Manolo for our own good. He was like a jasmine bush in bloom, making everybody light-headed. Rocío began playing with her hair the way she always did when she was being flirtatious. Courtney, ignored as she was at that moment, was sulking in a corner while sneaking glances at us.

I poured myself a drink.

I could tell Agustín was enjoying the woozy effect Manolo was having on everyone. We were behaving like a canasta club of old ladies who've been caught dipping into the cooking sherry. Drunk on sheer lust as I was, I don't think I cared much that Manolo's effect on me was so obvious to my long-time lover. Then Manolo broke the tension and turning to Agustín, he asked, Hombre, can one dance with her?

I looked up. Manolo's head was tilted in my direction. Everyone, including me, looked toward Agustín. Manolo asked in a way that in Spanish sounded coy and daring because it was so indirect you knew he had asked for something forbidden.

Just like Moctezuma when at last confronted by the man whom he did not think was a god, but a rival who believed the rumors of his own omnipotence, Agustín eyed Manolo like he knew that Manolo would not be stopped by anything. Agustín lit a cigarette, looked around for a moment and then he said, Why don't you dance with la Courtney?

Courtney stood up, but Manolo didn't turn her way. People got a little uncomfortable because of how easily Manolo had rebuffed Agustín's offer and no one ever did that to Agustín. The man was losing his touch. It set off sirens alerting all dogs and dissidents. The king is dead! they resounded.

Embarrassed by Manolo's dismissal, Courtney threw her long fringe shawl over her shoulders and went out the door, her footsteps fading a few minutes later with a certain cajón beat as she ran down the stairs.

My footsteps never sound like that, I thought.

We get compulsive about the darndest things. Mine is listening to the echo of my uneven footsteps.

The ensuing silence burned through us. I actually felt my hands grow cold as if the temperature in the room had just dropped. We all loved Agustín, were each indebted to him in some way, but he had this Hail, Caesar thing going on in his mind about himself so that all good citizens were left with no choice but to pray for his downfall.

Then José, his unfailing friend who obviously felt more compassion for Agustín than did the women in his life, started to play a siguiriya to thaw out the frost. I turned to the guitar and, smiling, began doing palmas. Like José's toque and Rocío's cante as she sipped a little cognac in between verses, Manolo moved slowly into his dance taking purposeful, sliding strides across the floor, gradually gathering heat from the lyrics and the guitar's jeremiad. Then, at I don't know what moment but like a spark in dry woods after no rain, José, Rocío and Manolo became a forest fire of sound and movement. All of our dilating irises were riveted on Manolo, who was a cyclone of white heat.

Doing palmas I was just sitting at first but then, as if Manolo had hypnotized me, I got up too and started slowly toward him, arms poised over my head. I forgot that I couldn't move like him, but it didn't matter, not to me nor to him. Our eyes stayed locked and whatever his gaze told me to do I did. In the background I could hear the guitar and Agustín's half-hearted olés and Rocío's beautiful cante and the bato's pitos but they were all far away. It was just me and Manolo somewhere. Maybe I am dancing over sand, I thought, that's why my feet are dragging, working harder than ever. Still I followed and still he led me out from the shore and then he took me in his arms for the first time, firm thin arms like tree vines. He wasn't much taller than me, we were staring almost eye to eye and when he spun me around it worked because I was not on the ground. I don't know how he became Baryshnikov all of a sudden, but he did. And then I landed back on my feet. My good one and my bad one without a sound, like a feather dropping, and for a moment I thought he might kiss me then and there but he didn't. Olé! called his bato, and Manolo smiled for the first time and I smiled too but didn't look at anyone, not at Agustín. Especially not at Agustín.

.   .   .

For a woman to know she is really loved she must draw a line in the ground that her lover is never permitted to cross. The line is not always the same and depends on the lover. With Agustín the line had been our pregnancy. I did not know that that was the line until afterward. I didn't even know about lines until then. But I did know that when he had crossed it he could not come back. No green card, no tariffs, just a one-way ticket out.

With Manolío, who was a personification on stage of a whirl-wind of fire, the line was our dancing. He knew before we even started that he should never let me fall or falter, never show me up. Maybe that was his true gift, to be that good and not show it off. It had to be like that, not because of my bad leg or my age and slow-ness compared to his vitality and youth, nor because he was just the best dancer alive ever born to flamenco. At least in my opinion. I had other qualities, fine body movements, graceful hands. I did a little castancts but not much because of the wrist pain. With me it was really the hands. They were my strength. But of course I couldn't move my feet very much.

But what I had was something else, what the Spanish call

"duende." The duende is something you are born with, soul to the blues. You can't buy it. Nobody can teach it to you. Manolo knew that I wouldn't dance with a splintered pata if I did not live for dancing too. I saw you had duende the night we met, Manolo told me. I knew it was you right away, ¡la famosa Carmen la Coja!

For the whole year we danced together he never crossed the dancer's line. But sometimes I wonder about other lines I might have drawn. Maybe Manolo would not have slipped away as smoothly as a silk shawl over bare shoulders. Other times I wonder if Manolo and I were never meant to do more than dance together. Between the lines.

chapter four

Uno: How do you like my haircut?

How do you like my haircut? my mother asked me tonight when I got in from my gaje gig at O'Hare. My pounding leg has me on pain pills all day now. That means I get around slower than usual. I'm being stubborn about using the new crutches while on the job. I just hobble back and forth behind the counter like a sorority girl with a leg in a cast from a ski accident. But en route I need the crutches. It's just been a few months since my summer power walks but now it's hard to imagine my getting to the bus stop on my own.

When I was a kid in the waif-like segunda garb Amá fitted me with, strangers were usually all too willing to assist the poor girl with the braced leg. They'd help me on the bus and give up their seat. One time a kindly lady gave me a dollar. Another time a lecher tried to drag me off with him, obviously mistaking my disability for stupidity, until I stomped him on the foot with my crutch. But now, at middle age, the waif look arouses little sympathy from most people on the streets of America for what appears to be just one more unlucky life.

In any case, I don't like strangers' attention. At least not the pitying kind.

As a dancer, even as a crooked one, I loved the adoration that *my* public gave me despite my malady. Sometimes I worried that it was really pity. But Manolo said no. It was my dance and only my dance. ¡Poderosa! he whispered in my ear after our first show together. Manolo had a way of flattering me without my feeling it was just flattery but the bona fide truth. A good lover will do that, see something worthwhile in you that you never knew was there. And when there's something you don't like to see in yourself a good lover won't see it either.

How's it look? Amá asks again about her new do. She's never worn any makeup but Amá has me dye her hair black-black every six weeks. The entire effect, now with the new hair cut, makes my little mother look like an Aztec horse jockey.

It looks good, I say. I put my crutches aside and sit down to pull off my boots.

I went to the barber where your father goes, she says, with a self-conscious stroke of the back of her shaved neck. Why pay more? You pay all this money at a beauty shop and they don't even do what you ask for!

She goes off to the kitchen pleased with her day's bargain. I'm still trying to get my boots off when I hear Amá add, You should go do something about your hair too, Carmen. The barber only charges eight pesos. My mother says "pesos" in Spanish but she means dollars.

I haven't cut my hair, really cut it, since high school. I trim the split ends myself. *If you loved me it was for my hair*, my favorite painting by Frida Kahlo reads. She cut her hair and immortalized her revenge against her bug-eyed rake of a husband with a self-portrait. *Now that I'm bald you don't love me anymore.*

You know what I think of a gitana cutting her hair. Agustín called me a gypsy woman every time I talked about being sick of dealing with long hair, especially in hot weather. People don't think of Chicago as having hot weather but it does.

I'm not a gitana, I'd say.

Yes, you are.

I couldn't concentrate with that black mane of yours, Manolo told me one evening after rehearsal. Me too with yours, I said.

Agustín. Manolo. Hair or not.

Maybe it's from stress but I think I'm shedding. Long black Carmen strands everywhere. Macho threw up a hairball the other day. It wasn't his hair the way a cat gets hairballs. It was mine. Macho's got this thing about going into wastebaskets to find things to chew. That's where he got my hair. I cured him of the habit right after that by wrapping up jalapeño peppers in tissue paper and sprinkling the trash with hot sauce. Amá didn't think it would work, but it did. Right away, too.

When Amá goes to bed Macho sleeps guarding her bedroom door. What's wrong with you, Macho? I say to the arthritic Chihuahua, trying not to let on how uneasy his diseased bared teeth make me whenever I try to check in on my mother. If your mistress dies because no one can get in to help her it's gonna be your fault, I whisper to him in Spanish. Macho doesn't understand English. *Perro-Macho!* I call him, macho and dog just rolling off my tongue together for some reason.

Amá has left a little plate on the stove for my cena. With a dollop of sour cream they are this side of heaven and I thank the stars for the little things in my life that have made it special: Amá's taquitos for sure. My music—el cante jondo. Manolo and me, of course. Oh, and my memories of Agustín, the good, the not so good, and the downright sad enough to disown. But I won't. Because they're mine. Sometimes when you take stock, memories are all you've got to call your own.

Dos: *Some men don't even like to do it . . .*

Some men don't even like to do it and Agustín was one of them, except when he was really drunk, and because nothing else was working he'd relent, and then I couldn't even pull him up for air. Usually I would be pretty drunk too, so that finally both of us being so worn out would go to sleep. For a long time I figured that there were just some places men have no business going.

I never even knew there were men who don't snore until Manolío fell asleep on me, even after they've been drinking—like we both had been that night when I finally had the nerve to bring him back to the Hollywood Hotel or Manolo had the nerve finally to invite himself.

It was the first occasion we were alone, or more precisely without Agustín, who had done one of his not-so-unusual disappearing acts that night. I'll be right back, he said while several of us were having drinks at the club where we performed. All right, everyone said or nodded, not bothering to even look up. But after a while with no Agustín we knew he had given us the slip again. The rest of us finished a couple of bottles of wine and then a couple more and then Manolo's bato said he felt tired and someone offered to give him a ride home because it was such a cold night. One by one, two by two, each left until at last it was just Manolo and me.

What's the matter, Manolío? I said, my speech a little slurred, not enough to sound sloppy but maybe just enough to be sexy. At least I hoped. No date tonight? I asked. Usually he'd have a female waiting in the wings. She'd sit at the bar feeling regal like the heiress apparent until he finished his business. You knew she was the one picked for that night because when she arrived they'd kiss the way he'd kissed me that first night at the party—a-hello-and-good-bye-with-everything-promised-in-between kiss, all at once. She'd sip a glass of wine all evening alone and finally he'd go over. Ready? his eyes would inquire as if she had not been exuding readiness for hours, but she would simply nod and he'd help her with her coat and out the door they'd go, arm in arm, letting in a blast of wind behind them. The next time I'd see Manolo it would be with someone else.

Instead of his customary cocky grin in response to such teasing, he laughed a little and stared into his empty glass like a fortune teller looking for an omen. That's when I knew what he was thinking. Thinking but not ever saying, never in front of the bato—who saw me as Agustín's woman and in any case not proper wife material for his son. I was an outsider and too old anyway for people who marry their daughters off right after puberty. It doesn't matter what country or what century, you do not marry outsiders without being ostracized. From Croatia to Italy, Granada to New York, India to Arizona, they were banded together with iron links of loyalty.

When we danced it wasn't a folkloric example of long-ago country customs. It was a glimpse through a tiny window for a few gold coins. I was allowed into that life through Agustín as a watered-down and, let's face it, inauthentic presentation of the gypsy woman for a public that he believed could not deal with the real thing. The real thing is not only too raw but too much of everything. And he did not believe the gaje-gringo audience bred on Hollywood wanted anything that real. I never was and never would be one of them. Manolo had not revealed his feelings for me in front of Agustín either, for obvious reasons. Why he chose to do it that night, I still don't know. Except that there are times when you finally give in to fate and it was time.

Where do you live anyway, Carmen? Manolo asked with a quick glance at me from the shade of his thick eyelashes. It took me a second to remember, between the wine and the look he was giving me, and then clearing my throat I answered, Oh yeah, the Hollywood Hotel on Wilson Avenue. If you think you can remember the address . . . would you like for me to take you home? he asked with a little chuckle. I laughed a little too but no sound came out.

We made our way through the near-abandoned streets of after-hours Chicago, snow falling lightly and sparkling like powdered sugar on the ugly harshness of asphalt as if we were in an old black-and-white movie. When I almost slipped Manolo took my hand, gripped it firmly and never let it go after that.

Once we got to my room he had to help me with the key. I

giggled a little nervously but tried to play it down and when I looked at him putting the key in I saw that he was nervous too. It should have been smoother, I thought, between two pros. He should have grabbed me up in his arms like he seemed ready to do when we first laid eyes on each other, like he had done a couple of times when we finished an especially good performance. He'd twirl me around and people would applaud harder and then he'd kiss me, the way dance partners kiss, with lips closed, quickly, and we would be smiling so hard you'd think our faces would break. Instead when we got inside he sat on my bed in his coat like a shy schoolboy. A kind of depressed shy schoolboy at that. That's when I knew he was in love with me.

Take your coat off! I said, aware of my slightly drunken speech sounding less sexy now than lascivious. The thought made me self-conscious and feel very tired next to those eyelashes and his pouting and all I could think was, What a mistake, what a mistake. I went to the cabinet for a couple of glasses, killed two cockroaches trying to escape, and decided to make an espresso on the hot plate to sober up instead of drinking anymore. What're you doing? he asked. I don't know, I said. It's too late for coffee, he said. I know, I said, but I think I'm drunk. I think you are too. No I'm not, he said. Yes you are, I said, feeling bad and drunk. Come here, he said. Come over here. I'll show you how drunk I'm not.

By the time I had shut the lights off and reached the bed Manolo had slipped out of his coat. He brought me close to him between his legs, me still standing, pulled my face down to his to kiss me. Then in one quick movement, my undergarments were gone and my skirt was up over my head and he had me spread before him like a Sunday brunch buffet. Not a position I objected to at all, I might add, even if my previous experience had not always given the desired results. I wrapped my thighs around Manolo's neck and drew him right in.

All the years I had been with Agustín had led me to believe that gypsy men weren't particularly eager about that act because they feared women could put a spell on men that way, a spell that would send them howling like wolves under black skies, a spell that would make their you-know-whats drop off the next time they tried to make love with any other woman, a spell of evil for life. Still, like I said, when he had drunk too much he'd do it as if he were doing me some great big favor.

But Manolo didn't do it like he was doing me a favor. He did it like he had dropped deep into the sea and knew exactly where the treasure was, small and precious and belonging to him and me, mostly me I was thinking when suddenly a gush I had never known, never believed could come from a woman poured forth. I thought my brains had blown out of my head at the same time—shot out through my skull, gone out the window and landed on the blinking neon light of the Hollywood Hotel. Then Manolo moved up to me, his under-the-sea voice repeating my name in my ear into the damp space between my neck and shoulder into the spray of my hair over the pillow again and again not like a chant not sweet or hypnotic or mystical but terrible and low, terrible and low like everything would always be between us. But that first night I welcomed our wet birth like a calf in a barn born just before light. It was still ours to do with as we would choose, to sustain us or to sacrifice for the greater cause. For a long time after Manolo fell asleep I lay awake repossessing my soul bit by bit, my head against the satin of Manolo's chest.

When I woke up the next day he was gone.

I looked around my room as if he could possibly be hiding anywhere in a one-room studio. No note of course. Calorros aren't into writing.

Later he called.

Why did you leave? I asked. I was really shaken up by self-doubt but I didn't let on. I don't sleep well if I'm not in my own bed, you know? he said. Then he laughed. Manolío the alley cat. I wasn't even sure he had a bed of his own anywhere. It was a good answer but not the truth. Truth in the case of my lovers always being a matter of opinion.

Tres: Loving Manolo—Manolío—was
thrusting both hands out . . .

Loving Manolo—Manolío—was thrusting both hands out into the darkness to clutch onto something more than numinous air but also hoping that whatever it was won't bite you. Mi Manolío was dark, even in winter, his skin savory and sweet like Mexican chocolate that makes your mouth water just to whiff it simmering and waiting for you on the stove to have with birthday cake. Manolo was a birthday cake with exactly twenty lit candles when we met. A cake not quite done yet. And I was the birthday girl surprised in the dark.

Manolo's bato was a violinist from Yugoslavia. His mother danced. She was born in Mexico, he said, but her family came from Spain. Manolo himself came into the world in New York where his parents met at a big gypsy campout for St. Agnes. So are you Spanish or Mexican? I asked one night, looking into his eyes as if there were a fixed location in them. Dark pecan eyes roasted almost black. Were his roasted pecan eyes Serbian or Sevillan? In the end maybe

Manolo was just another all-American boy with high ambitions. Only a little goat-flavored.

I don't get you, I finally said, looking at him hard. I was looking and looking but I couldn't figure him out. All I know is that I dance, Manolo shrugged. Unlike Agustín who had answers for everything, even instantly invented ones, Manolo just sometimes brushed big questions off. The small ones all the time.

He held up five fingers in the shadows of my room as we lay together that night. I've got five passports, he said. Don't ask me where I got them. I gave him a gentle push against the shoulder. He fell back. He fell back and then he straightened up again and said, That's how I get around. And wherever I'm going next I'll just get there. But none of that means who I am.

I myself believed Manolo was calorro through and through. The gypsy belongs to the entire world although the world over disowns the gypsy, Agustín said about the Rom diaspora. And Manolío felt unwanted everywhere he went and he was unwanted everywhere he went.

Except by me. *I* wanted him—that Byzantine finger-snapping boy.

My Muslim-Christian-Jewish saint of sacrilegious yearnings,

Indo-Pakistani with at least one line of maybe Otomí American blood

going through his throbbing veins.

My gypsy gazelle sleepy-eyed dreamer whom if I could dream I would have dreamed up—I

wanted all of him.

The first time he ever saw me naked was the first time I told Manolo I loved him. I did not ever plan on telling him that I loved him. Enough women had loved him and told him and would love him yet and tell him. It was enough that I loved him my own way without saying it. But once when dawn stretched its fingers toward the bed, sheets on the floor, my threadbare nightclothes on the bedpost like white flags of surrender, before I opened my eyes he opened his so that I did not get the chance to reach for cover to hide my long bent stick of a leg, the foot curved like a beggar's hand. Then he muttered half-asleep with eyes barely open, *Bella*. My sleeping beauty.

He reached over and began to tickle me from neck to toe, tickled me all over, and without thinking but only feeling I called out, Te quiero Manolo, te quiero, as a way of surrender. *Te quiero* means I want you/like you a lot/but not exactly love you, and then he looked me in the eyes and without realizing I was going to say it I said, Te amo, which only means I love you, because I did.

.　.　.

Among my people, Manolo said on another night of nakedness and baring souls, everyone came out to see me. When Manolo and I were out or around others we didn't say much to each other. But alone we talked all the time. By the time I was fourteen I was a star, Manolo said, a star that shines but is in another galaxy so you here on earth don't see it. At fourteen, for us, you are a man already. Ready to start a family. All I ever wanted was to dance. Do you know I once was asked to dance in Hong Kong by a descendent of a monarch? Manolo smiled. Manolo had the best smile but not the best laugh. When he laughed it sounded more like, Watch out.

Manolo told me his Chinese story. Because of communism, the royal family was forced to work in the rice paddies but they had inherited aristocratic tastes. They hid their heirlooms in a cave way up in the mountains. He gave me a pendant, Manolo said, making an O with his index finger and thumb, made of elephant tusk. The family seal was carved into it. A big ferocious bear. It was magnificent but I gave it away . . . to a girl. She had eyes like two lines and skin like that paper you use to trace with, you know? She was so pretty but poor, poor. She asked me for it. It made me feel like a king to give a gift like that away, but I regretted it afterward. Especially now when I would have given it to you.

Magnificent pendant lost to a rice-paddy girl. I believed Manolo's stories of dancing magnificence because in front of me Manolo was magnificent. You can say that about a dancer, call him magnificent if he is and not sound crazy. Crazy in love. I danced before I learned to walk, he said. He had been given everything at one time or another and everything slipped away, came back in other shapes and forms.

Manolío my prize. The sparkling pinky diamond on the bato's finger, and he was the only thing that meant anything to his father following Manolo's mother's death one night in a car accident. It wasn't in China but on some other faraway road. Maybe if I hadn't spoiled him so much he would have worked harder, Manolo's bato told Agustín. What does he think? Manolo said to me, but not to his father. Never to his father. That dancing is not hard work? At seven years old my dancing supported our whole family! I never knew what it was to play, to have friends my own age!

Whenever Manolo came to see me at the Hollywood Hotel he'd bring a little gift. What gives some lovers the guasa to think it's all right to show up empty-handed at a woman's door as if their you-know-whats in tow were enough is beyond me. *Guasa* means ATTI-TUDE, and if you've ever seen a gypsy decked out and ready for the night, you know what guasa means. Enough to make a Latin lover pale in comparison. Almost.

Once Manolío brought a bag of cashews wrapped with a red ribbon. I wasn't a big nut fan but after that I couldn't eat a cashew without thinking of him.

Another time he brought something very curious to my terrestrial eyes. It's a sand dollar, he said. Be careful. I took it in both hands and it cracked in half. But when you put it together there's a kind of flower embossed on it. Something used to live in it, I think. It's on my dresser now stuck together with Super Glue. I found it myself, Manolo said. Diving in the Canary Islands. I thought gypsies didn't swim, I told him. Why do you say that? he asked with that dry laugh of his. Oh, because of Agustín? Agustín's just afraid of water. Manolo acted as if it was me acting foolish instead of Agustín.

Up until then Agustín had represented all his people to me. If he didn't like beer it was because gypsies didn't drink beer. If he kept out of deep water it was a gypsy fear. That's when I learned that with every culture there are two sides. If you believe one thing to be true about a people the very opposite will also be true. At that moment it became very clear to me that my two lovers were two faces of the same ancient coin. I was very happy.

Because his fetish was music, Manolo brought lots of cassette tapes, music from the many places where he had visited, music we danced to—from Algiers and Tangier, Morocco and Mexico—music to make love to.

Whenever he showed up unexpectedly, which after knowing him awhile became predictable—when the bar had closed, Agustín had declared the end of the night and went on his own way, or money had run out—Manolo would bring one long-stemmed crimson rose. Once when I was angry and refused to answer the door,

Manolo left his offering behind. It was January and winter even in my hallway so that by morning the rose had frozen and stuck to the gritty floor. When I picked it up its outline was still there.

Maybe it's true what Agustín spat out one night at me, that all Manolo looked for in me was the mother he had lost as a boy. So what? If I could have Manolo back for one day I would be his mother. I would be his mother and his lover too. I would hold him and feed him and kiss his brow good-night at bedtime. I'd read him the German fairy tales that he loved so much, that he didn't even know of until me.

I read everything to Manolo and he wanted to hear me read everything. He didn't like to read, not in any of the three or four languages he spoke. He didn't like to listen to the radio either, like I did everyday. Too much talking, he'd say. But he wanted me to tell him whatever I heard, especially about what used to be Yugoslavia or maybe still is except that it got cut up like a T-bone steak for some-body's dinner. It was where his father's people were. It's everybody's tragedy, Manolo told me, not just for the gypsies but for Christians and Muslims and Macedonians and Bosnians. Names dropped out of his mouth that sounded like kingdoms in a very bleak legend where instead of children and pregnant women being swallowed by one-eyed giants and fire-breathing dragons, they were speared and gutted by soldiers with bayonets. Because Muslims believe in Allah, he said, they were swept up by bulldozers and dumped in a river to drown. The river filled up and became peat moss with so many bodies soaking it up. You won't read that anywhere, my lover said, tell me if you do. His roasted-pecan eyes got watery and so did mine. Manolo could do that to me. Have me turn on the waterworks by just telling me a story, maybe because his stories were all true.

I felt foolish with my tales because I knew then that their happy endings were only a cover-up for what really must've happened back then, and what really happened you don't want to know, he'd say. But I did. I wanted to know everything he had heard through his own channels, labyrinths of passed-on Romany mutterings, a caló telegraph wire stretched across a large land mass, a lament, wail, a conch-shell warning from seashore to seashore. I wanted to know about Manolo's grandparents, about his four uncles and three aunts and their children and grandbabies who had survived everything, eating garbage, living in trailers and shanties and scorned by all, who had escaped it all. Especially what I needed to know was whether it was true, what I heard Manolo's father talking about one night with Agustín but stopping when I was in earshot— that people were buried alive because of these so-called ethnic cleansings. And you know, compai, our people are nothing to them, I heard the old man whisper between clenched teeth. His arched white eyebrow seemed to point toward his son, who was sitting next to him. He's a crazy boy, he said. He's bound to go back there to see who's all right . . .

Cuatro: That October—my only
October with Manolo—

That October—my only October with Manolo—was so rich with melancholy that although we hadn't had a gig for a while we didn't care. When my body was up to it we spent our afternoons taking walks along the beach. Not too many big cities have their own lakes. We liked our lake a lot. The Mediterranean-Lite, Manolo called it. He said it looked like the Mediterranean Sea, filled with so many little boats and so blue on sunny days and with its heavy waves signaling winter's approach. But of course it's only a little lake, he'd laugh, teasing me because I had never seen any sea firsthand and for me Lake Michigan was big enough.

Ah! Manolo said, gajes here in America think that everything they have is bigger than whatever anyone else has!

Ah! I said back, but you and I know that's not always the case, is it? And Manolo looked at me, caught off-guard for a second by my entendre, then laughed.

Once, he ripped off half of his clothes, threw off his shoes and socks and dived in on a dare. You owe me, Carmen! he yelled, climbing out, shivering like a wet dog. I couldn't believe he had jumped into the cold lake on a dollar bet. I'll make you dinner, how's that? I offered, feeling a little sorry for him. No, I want the dollar, he said. He put back on his clothes, which clung to his wet body since he hadn't dried himself off, and took my dollar. He kissed it, said something under his breath that seemed like a prayer, and put it in his pocket. This is for our son, he said. Hmm, I said.

It was while sitting in the park on a bench on one of those moody autumn days, resting and Manolo rubbing my leg a little, that he said, Why don't we have a child together? Are you crazy, I said. Crazy for you, he said.

I hadn't thought about babies for a long time. My spine had gotten worse than it was when I was pregnant at twenty-five. It probably was not a good idea but I liked it. Autumn will do that to you, have you feeling nostalgic for things you never had. I studied Manolo's face for a little while. If our baby looked like you, he'd be a heartbreaker! I said.

A heartbreaker like his mother! Manolo snorted. He got up and picked up a few pebbles and began throwing them one by one. He hit a squirrel by accident, right in the head. It fell over. Did you kill it? I gasped. How horrible, Manolo, you killed that little animal!

Manolo squinted. No, it's just stunned, he said. A few seconds later the squirrel got up and ran off. I don't think of myself as a heartbreaker, I said.

But you are, Carmen, Manolo said. He stopped throwing pebbles and looked at me. That's the worst kind of heartbreaker, one who doesn't even know she's doing it!

I really didn't know what Manolo was talking about. I was very sincere with him. If I hadn't broken up with Agustín, although I hardly saw him around lately, it was because Manolo wouldn't let me tell him about us. He didn't want to hurt his godfather's feelings, Manolo said.

I looked up and shaded my eyes from the sun's glare behind him. He looked like a boy in silhouette. He was not a boy but sometimes he was fragile like one. He didn't want me to hurt Agustín, but obviously he didn't want to get hurt either. Who does? Sometimes, as tough and man-of-the-world as Manolo was at such a young age, he was as delicate as Venetian glass with swirls of gold leaf painted on. I wondered if I was delicate in his eyes too, even if only now and then, when we danced on stage, for instance, or when he woke at dawn and I was still sleeping and he ran his hand over the sheet along the length of my torso down to my thighs. Half asleep, I could feel my own shape, as if his hand caressing me like that were shaping me into a beautiful woman. God made man and woman in His own image, so what He made were a pair of androgynes, I figured. Plato said the androgynes divided in two and became man *and* woman. With his touch Manolo separated me from him. When together, we felt whole, were both divine.

How could we have a child? I said. We don't even live together.

And? he asked. Do you think because you have one room in one place and I in another that we don't share everything already?

Cinco: My mother says she may be having a heart attack . . .

My mother says she may be having a heart attack, I say to the young Puerto Rican woman with a silver ring on her thumb working behind the glass partition at the reception desk. We still have to go through filling out all the forms and some waiting, but fortunately for the most part they got it straight at the emergency ward that when you say heart attack it's not prudent to have you take a number like they have almost everyone else do. Other old ladies who woke up their daughters in the middle of the night but weren't shrewd enough to yell heart attack like my amá did, but insisted that they are only having heartburn, trying not to alarm anyone, remain in the waiting room dying a heroic death.

Macho's hysterical yapping woke me or maybe it was my mother's cries at 3 A.M. that seemed to be coming from far, far away when suddenly I sat right up like Frankenstein's monster when he got that vital jolt. I knew right away it wasn't a nightmare but something awful and real. There were times in my life when being real did not necessarily mean awful. But lately they've become inseparable.

After I return the clipboard to the registration desk Amá is directed to a narrow room where a nurse takes her vitals. I . . . can't . . . breathe, Amá tells the nurse. What medication are you on, dear? the nurse asks and starts to take my amá's blood pressure.

My mother's English is being frightened away by what I call panic of the gringo, because instead of answering she waves a hand at her vinyl purse, which I'm clutching. Clutching while leaning against a wall. In the commotion of getting my jefita to the hospital as quickly as possible I not only didn't bring my crutches, but because I took an extra dose of painkillers before bed I am also a little groggy. I open the purse, but from the looks on both women I'm not moving quickly enough for anybody. The nurse stops what she's doing and gives me a once-over. You'd think she never saw a medicated cripple in a flannel nightgown before. I'm starting to get a little sweaty. After I give the nurse the prescriptions I limp away to find an available chair in the waiting room.

It's noisy and dirty and very active in the emergency room. Three bloody gangbangers curse up a storm while waiting to be attended to, plan out their revenge in the barrio, ghetto, projects, West Side, South Side, North Side, suburbia, wherever it is they claim their turf, in between putting the make on sick women. Meanwhile, a steady stream of inner-city horrors keeps flowing in. A parade of not one, not two, but four girls in wheelchairs. I do mean girls, just babies, babies with big hair, really tiny things with baggy pants and the smallest round bellies protruding through their oversize plaid shirts, who are off to deliver their elfin offspring. One has a boyfriend, a slender boy-man with a tough strut and big shoes pushing the wheelchair, but the rest are pushed by their mothers, all of whom look younger than me and who are about to become grandmothers before the night is through.

A deafening ringing starts up in my head. Where is time going? it says. Where is time going? I don't know this city of violent youth killing for kicks, playing Russian roulette, as I hear one boy brag to another about, at a sweet-sixteen party. What kind of sweet-sixteen party is that? Everyone was high, the boy says, the gun went around until finally one got it. Bam! Man! It blew everybody's high!

I almost had a baby at twenty-five. Here there are babies being born tonight, maybe every night, to babies living for the next killer high—maybe it's bashing in someone's head with a steering-wheel lock, maybe it's sniffing an aerosol can and going into a coma, maybe it's a bullet to the head, bam man it blows everybody's high!

I never knew this life. The children I went to school with would have been juiced just to wake up one morning with all their senses intact. What they wouldn't have done to hear, see, think clearly for one day; to get up and walk, Rise! like Jesus said, and they'd get up and make their bed, and have some oatmeal and get ready for school, no one having to carry them on and off the toilet or saying, C'mon, Beto, hurry up, I'm in a hurry too. Dag, man! Are you finished yet? Can you reach the toilet paper or do you need help with that too?

This was not the city I knew as a young woman when I went out in it, to its dimly lit hopping bars and hip restaurants. Dancing was my kick once when I could hardly walk. For a few bucks a night I danced. For free brandy I danced. I drank a little too much per-haps. Maybe it was my own kind of recklessness. But we were stoned on music, eternal songs and rhythms and yes, profound love. Not just a love you couldn't have but love for a land you've lost, longing for a place to rest and mothers we missed and times past never to be regained. We got loaded on longing.

Suddenly the teen warriors start to fade. I got this ringing in my head that no one else around me seems to hear. Great, I'm hearing voices now, I think. Of course, why not? Between the voices and abstinence, my caring for the aged and my life of poverty, I'll be beatified any day now. My leg throbs worse than ever. Take another pain pill, no I can't, not yet. When I bend over to rub it I get this sudden sinking feeling that my life has been ripped from under me, a generation has gone and my city at night is no longer exciting and grand but now a veritable battle front. The young are being taken down in alleys and parks. Who declared this war on our children? This isn't *The Lord of the Flies,* this isn't Serbia or Zaire or Medellín. This is Chicago, my city, America the Free! Isn't it? Isn't it? I just do not have a grip on things anymore, do not have a grip, but who could say if I ever did, sheltered crippled dancer that I was, romantic that I am, and as far as I can tell, that's what makes the world go 'round and 'round. And then my body falls head-first and I can't remember what happens next.

Seis: It's just like the story my yoga instructor once . . .

It's just like the story my yoga instructor once told the class, years ago, when I could still sit on the floor and bend over. Although we are dying from the moment of birth, we're like the frog that is being swallowed by the snake, he said. Even as the frog is being swallowed, it's flicking tongue is trying to catch a fly. After Amá was finally admitted that long night, she was injected, put on an IV and at last seen by a drowsy intern on duty who did nothing more than ask about her prescriptions before saying there was nothing to do now until the morning when my mother's doctor would come see her. I patted her hand and said don't worry and I saw it in her eyes—

her indomitable will to live. It was nearly morning when I dragged myself through the less than antiseptic corridors and out the door.

Amá's apartment was eerie without her, just Macho sniffing on the other side of the door as I fit the key in a double-bolt lock like the one I had installed at the Hollywood Hotel. It was once a symbol of being an independent woman. Now it's just a protection device for those who live in fear.

Not much protection either, since somehow Negrito got in and I find him sleeping in my mother's bed. Macho jumps up next to him and snuggles under his arm like a teddy bear. How is she? my baby brother whom I haven't seen since who-knows-when asks in the semidarkness without opening his eyes. She'll be okay, I say. What're you doin' here?

Don't worry, Negrito says, I ain't sticking around. He sits up. He use to be the pretty son, but now his eyes are abandoned and his hair has thinned from overconsumption of illegal and legal drugs. He's so spare his pants look like nobody's in them. He's also a little dirtier than usual.

How long have *you* been here? he asks me back. A year, huh? ¡Pobre de ti! he says sarcastically and lays back down. I grab and throw Macho the snarling dog on the floor to lay down next to my brother. I like to lie on my stomach. You're tired, huh? he says, throwing an arm over me like a roller-coaster bar that keeps you from plunging to your death. I nod. If you need some money, I say, I got a little for you but don't mess with Amá's stuff, all right? Don't worry, Negrito says, patting me on the butt. Remember when we use to fool around? he asks. Uh-huh, I say. By the way, I wonder, did I turn you gay?

Oh puh-lease, mi'ja! Negrito says and we both go to sleep.

In the morning when I wake, Negrito's gone without a trace, barely an imprint left on the bed. I'm a little ashamed of myself to make a house inspection anyway. Of course Negrito didn't take anything from home. He never does.

chapter five

Uno: Corazón de melón . . .

Corazón de melón de melón melón melón corazón . . . *de melón* is the jumpy chachachá my jefitos danced to when they were still young and in love. My jefito comes up whistling it softly when my mother is in the hospital. In those memories of when my parents were still in love, I could not dance. I had just come out of the hospital and was in a wheelchair. But I remember my apá at a party once picking me up to dance a Pérez Prado mambo with him. He was dashing then, with a pencil-thin mustache like the one worn by Pedro Infante, who looked more like a crooning garage mechanic than a movie idol.

Apá worked a lot of overtime back in the days when this was a great country for laborers and you could get time-and-a-half for working past your forty hours, not like companies are doing now, allowing foreign children to work as slaves because on their shoulders rests their families' survival, children who were unlucky to be born in countries that don't have labor laws. Apá worked overtime a lot, as I said, and also got home even later from the tavern where he had the custom of stopping off, so that it was way past supper time and we were usually in bed when he came rolling home.

Leave that child alone! "Creature" is actually what she called me in Spanish. That's okay. In English children are *kids*. Amá, who had been pretending she was asleep until then, would yell from her bedroom when she knew he had come into my room and was waking me up. Sometimes he'd just give me a hug and say, I'm sorry, mi'jita, I'm sorry!, weeping a little and rocking me. He thought God was punishing him for something by giving me polio. Other times he'd put a record on and get himself happy, Amá having a fit from her bed but refusing to get up, trying to pretend he wasn't acting stupid and drunk but at last yelling at him that he was. For the children's sake, would you come to bed now! He'd play a mambo or a danzón or a rumba because my apá besides working hard could really dance. Get up! he'd say to her. Come dance with me, vieja! "Old woman" being the way my father affectionately addressed his wife. Okay, then, mi'jita will dance with me, he'd say. I wanted to dance, only I couldn't, so he'd pick me up and carry me to the living room and we'd dance like that, rumba or mambo or real slow cheek-to-cheek, me smelling the beer on his breath and the rough of his nubby face, him whistling to debonair Nat King Cole.

I know it's no coincidence that the men I loved later were dancers. You don't have to be Freud to figure that much out. It's what I admired most, what was most out of reach because of my leg and yet within my reach because of love.

. . .

I have earlier, pre-polio memories, memories of when I walked right and dance wasn't everything. Not memories exactly, not snapshot recollections, but three-second mental reels like a dream; those Kodak family home movies that we could not afford I have preserved in the archives of my gray matter. My mother is the leading lady of my earliest recollections. I am on her knee and she is tickling, tickling me. I'm a little monkey, head upside down, a new baby clone, her hope perhaps and inspiration. Maybe not. Maybe I was just a surprise like my aunt used to say about her youngest-born. I thought Junior was a tumor! Can you imagine my surprise! By the time I realized I was pregnant—it was too late! *Too late?* Junior, my cousin, and I looked at each other wondering what "too late" meant.

I look up and Amá, who was a girlish pretty Mamita then, is smoking a cigarette. I've never known my mother to smoke but in that scene she brings a cigarette up to her red-colored mouth and takes a nice long puff. Her ebony hair with its shiny undulations is swept up in a long ponytail. She looks glamorous. When she presses me to her chest, I am caught up in that inimitable smell of Mamita sensuality, but I'm a child so I can only compare it then to a Vick's rubdown when you have a cold, only better. In another reel, which I have played in many a dark hour since, Amá has a new camera. Apá gave it to her for Christmas. Smile, mi'jita, she is calling to me. I'm barefoot and in a dirty romper. I smile with two teeth and chocolate all over my face. Is that a memory or does she have that picture somewhere? In yet another we are all going to Mass. My two big brothers in their First Holy Communion suits are walking in front of us as somber as a pair of Black Muslims. My baby brother and I are alongside Amá. I'm in the middle. I get to hold both hands. Amá says to someone, maybe the priest after Mass, Yes, this is our princess. She's growing up too fast! The memory reels all burn out during my illness and only come back erratically afterward, sporadic frames in which I'm not sure what happened, what I've dreamed and where I've filled in the blanks.

.   .   .

Macho waves his tail at my father, then he waddles off to lie down on an old throw rug. How are the new crutches working out? my apá asks. No one else in the family has brought up the fact that after all these years I'm back to crutches. Okay, I say. My jefito has a look on him like Macho's. He's seemed defeated ever since Amá made him leave. I don't want to add to his worry about my mother so I don't elaborate on what the doctor has told me lately, that I am showing definite indications that the polio is back. The crutches are only the first sign of what is appearing to be my fate. If the truth be known, I haven't quite accepted the doctor's word as gospel myself.

My father, who is the younger of the two, looks worse than my mother, but he hasn't been to a doctor I'd guess since his induction exam during the Korean War, before I was born. He didn't pass, for some banal reason no one would have ever thought of, like flat feet. He comes from the school of thought that going to doctors is what makes you sick.

Would you like something to eat? I ask Apá. Not that I'm about to do any cooking but I'm sure my mother left a pot of beans in the refrigerator. No respectable Mexican home in the North is ever without a pot of pinto beans and flour tortillas.

He shrugs his shoulders. He's still in his work clothes, the thermal jacket with a torn pocket. He's carrying his metal lunch pail. I'll just get going, he says, not looking at me. If his demeanor gets any more pathetic I'll start crying. Do you think your amá wants me to go visit her? he asks at the door.

You know she'd never forgive you if you didn't! The lie just slips out because I don't want to be my amá's accomplice in hurting people's feelings. He was always nice enough, if not much more could be said of him as a father. He's always worked, too. Apá used to bring home all his pay until she threw him out. He still comes over on Fridays like clockwork and gives her a good share of it for the house bills.

Come down to eat later! Apá says. My father's specialty is chorizo and eggs. He looks over his shoulder, adds, You look too skinny, hija. You gotta take care of yourself. You gonna disappear.

No such luck. I've already tried that. Sometimes you get to feeling so lousy you want to will yourself away, fade out like an old photograph or a hologram, you were there but not really. Suicide seems too self-serving, too crass. Too sudden. I like drama, but live, preferably on stage. Something about a grand final exit doesn't appeal to me as much as the idea of being asked for an encore.

So I'm still here.

And someday, believe it or not, I'm sure I'll hear the applause that will call me out for one last time.

*Dos: Shadowy and looming, bright
and gloomy . . .*

Shadowy and looming, bright and gloomy, is how I would describe my brother, Abel, a divorced man with no social life and no aspirations but to keep up with current events. For what purpose, who knows, since he doesn't talk much to anyone. No friends to speak of, doesn't even bowl. Why bowl? I don't know. It just seems like a good way to make friends, something my brother Abel does not do.

As usual during our brief encounters, he startles me when I wake up on the couch and find him standing over me. I can't say how often he's done that. There's the latest *Time* and *Newsweek*, he says on his way to the kitchen, referring to the pile of magazines he brought home from the newsstand. I watch my brother's gelatin-like body aim for the kitchen. How's Amá? he shouts as I hear the refrigerator door open. Like my jefitos, he can't ask anything potentially emotional face-to-face. She's okay now, I think! I yell back, and trying to sit up and straighten my clothes I wonder why my brother has always given me the willies just a little bit. He comes back to the living room with a cold plate of leftovers. I'm worried about our mother, he says. He sits down in our parents' favorite chair in front of the big TV and begins to eat while watching The Weather Channel. He'd never come over and do all this if Amá were home. Sure, we're all brave when she's not around. If you're so worried about her why don't you go see her in the hospital? I ask. Our five minutes of niceties are over and our lifetime of sibling rivalry is back. He'd box the ears on Dumbo, my stuffed toy elephant, then I'd wait for him to go out to play so that I could take apart his electric train set, leave it out in the alley, piece by piece. Even my polio didn't stop our attacks.

I watch my brother finishing up his meal, which he didn't bother to warm up, not even in the microwave that Apá won in a raffle at work. He takes a bite of tortilla rolled up in one hand, which he did heat up on the burner because even the biggest jerk in the world knows not to eat a tortilla cold—except for the gringo-gajes. They just don't know better. I was at a benefit once where I was invited to dance with Agustín. It was a fund-raiser for Guatemala or Nicaragua, someplace in Central America back when a generation of Americans were so upset that their country had been causing so much trouble there for most of the twentieth century. They passed a plate of cold tortillas around to eat with your food like they were big Communion wafers. Ugh! I wish someone would tell them, I whispered to Agustín because I was hungry and refused to eat pinto beans mixed with couscous or maybe it was brown rice, it was hard to tell as the lukewarm casserole dish went by. What for? said Agustín, who was always so picky about food that he wasn't eating anything that was being passed around anyway.

I did already, my brother finally answers in reply to my question about visiting Amá, and I can tell he considers it harassment that I even asked. *You did?* I feel foolish having doubted him but still surprised that he actually went to the hospital. Yeah, but she wasn't there. She wasn't there? I ask. Where could she have gone? She's *in* the hospital! They said they had taken her down for some X-rays or something. X-rays? For what? I say. This is too much. I'm sure he didn't go now. Of course he didn't go. He never goes. After a moment of heavy silence he says, Did you hear about the raids at the Dollar Mart down in Little Village? Little Village is loaded with Chicago Mexicans and Mexican Mexicans. Who can tell them apart? Not the INS. There have been rumors of immigration raids at many of the businesses there in recent months. Most of the employees at Dollar Mart are maybe making minimum wage, if that. They don't all have documents. But some do. They all got taken in anyway, Abel says. Yeah, I say. It's awful. Yeah, he says, they're just scapegoats for big-time interests. People treated like dispensable machinery. My useless brother actually talks like that, like a political commentator on public television. Yeah, I say, I can't stand to think about it. I know, he says. Me neither. Then he gets up to get a second helping.

Tres: *While Amá is in the hospital I commit a mortal sin.*

While Amá is in the hospital I commit a mortal sin. I clean out her refrigerator. To the best of my knowledge this hasn't been done since July 20, 1969, the day Neil Armstrong set foot on the moon. Funny how world events serve to remind you of the most trivial things that nevertheless, having to do with your own little life, have left a greater impression on you than world history. If a man can go to the moon, I remember my mother saying, I can find out what's in the back of my refrigerator.

I catch the flu and have to stay home from work for two days when it occurs to me that with my amá's diabetes worsening, I really need to keep a closer eye on her. Abel comes up when I have taken out and laid on the table all the frying pans and pots with lids and serving spoons stuck inside, stored by Amá. Oh my God, I don't want to be here when Amá gets home, he said and left right away although my mother at that moment was lying a safe distance away in her adjustable hospital bed.

A broken shelf has been rigged with a stick and rolls of newspaper.

I take a peek in the freezer and decide that's a job for another day.

There are old catsup bottles and expired salsa jars and various containers of recycled lard, black calcified serrano chiles and fossilized limes, old packets of soy sauce and Chinese mustard in a plastic bag from the days when my jefitos got in a routine of ordering takeout on Fridays when Amá still worked at the factory and they could splurge like that.

I scrub all the shelves and trays. I get out a box of new Tupperware from the stash that we give to Amá every Mother's Day and that goes unused. There's a peculiar homemaker thrill whenever I get to fill one up just exactly right. After I'm done, I stand back and admire my glorious achievement. Like Neil Armstrong, I want to plant a flag and claim the new frontier in the name of peace.

All the while I know I'm in for it. The clear blue Tupperware—innocent enough in someone else's refrigerator—looks like Attila the Hun's army invading my mother's turf.

Still, I forge ahead. Later, I replace the fruit punch beverages with real grapefruit juice. Remove all salt shakers from the spice shelf and the salt packages from the pantry. Bring in fresh produce and donate the canned goods to the Uptown soup kitchen. I am happy and proud to do all of this for my mother, who is very sick and who might have died if I had not gotten her into the hospital on time and who, I'm sure, will know how much she is cared for by me, not her best child, perhaps not her favorite, but one who loves her the same, as awkwardly as my walk but just the same.

My flu gets worse and I miss a third day of work and cannot pick up my mother from the hospital the day she is released. My father has to take the afternoon off—akin to a venial sin for Mexicans. He also doesn't want to hear what she'll say when she opens the refrigerator, so my apá leaves as soon as she's settled.

As it turns out, my mother doesn't say a word about it. But as the weeks go by, whenever I offer to clean up the kitchen, she turns me down. I'll do it, she says with an air of suspicion that starts to make me feel a little like Bette Davis in *Baby Jane*. The pans return. The pots with lids and spoons left in. The salt, too, eventually finds its way back to the kitchen with a vengeance.

My mother begins losing weight on her new diet. My daughter isn't letting me eat, she whispers Joan Crawfordishly on the phone to one of my aunts one day. I'm going to disappear! Eventually she starts sneaking out on foot to do her own food shopping to subvert my fat-free, sugar-free, low-sodium, low in carbohydrates, organic, well-meaning purchases, which are left to rot in the refrigerator and pantry. That's okay, you eat them, she tells me.

When I go to work, she cooks up a fat feast like I've not seen since I was a child, an even further regression back to the Depression Era–style food she grew up with: fried chitlins, pig's feet, neck bones with collard greens in hot chile sauce. I find them stiffened in cold salsa or lard in their pots and pans in the refrigerator.

Why don't you ever bring home any more of those apple tarts from work for me like you used to? she asks me with a tone more of accusation than request.

They're not good for you, I say.

One isn't going to hurt! I like eating those kinds of things in the morning. They help get me started. I'm always feeling so tired all day.

You're tired from the medication and because you eat those kinds of things, I tell her.

Humph! she says under her breath. I feel tired anyway.

The next time I go to work I remember. Against my better judgment I pick up an apple tart on the way home. Amá is happy. Between Amá being a little happy, at least momentarily, with eating whatever she craves and me being made very unhappy, not just by her resistance to changing her diet because she says that it's all too late anyway, but because she sees me as conspiring against her happiness, I've taken the road with less flak. I've also come to believe that it isn't selfish to do so.

When did my mother become such an old woman?

When did I stop being a young one?

My mother has shrunken to a small pellet of a human being before my eyes and I didn't even see it happen. Her arms have shriveled like cucumbers in vinegar. Yet I know it is my mother because that is still her voice, the same one that, whatever it demands of me, I never question. Well, I may question it but I don't defy her openly, dare to confront the same sonorous voice that once sang like a bird nested in her throat as she rolled out the dough for her Saturday-morning tortillas when I was a little girl, that has given me my love for song.

When, for God's sake, did my mother stop singing?

One night when I am tossing and turning over it, I come to the conclusion that my conscience is clear. Unable to sleep, worrying about what Amá's doctors have told us, that one day she may have to go on a dialysis machine, I experience a revelation, a garden-variety enlightenment, and I know I cannot feel bad about Amá anymore. I must let go of the guilt for having failed her now, failed her so well without even trying, without even knowing how I did it, while she still sleeps soundly in the next room. And the following morning I come to terms with myself, the defective daughter that I am, inside and out, and realize that if I have not always felt Amá's love, I've loved myself enough for the two of us.

Cuatro: The Ides of March blew terrifying . . .

The Ides of March blew terrifying winds and rain across the Midwest plains during early spring this year. Saturday I worked as usual and just barely made it home, not becuase of the weather but because I was as slow as a sand-digging turtle. I'd hardly made it through the day, between the airport crowd, the demand for pizzas, drinks and frozen yogurt twirls, and we were one person short on a heavy travel day, which translated to one constant rush. By evening it felt as though my left thigh had atrophied.

But on Monday when I went to see the doctor she said my muscles didn't simply *feel* atrophied, that is what appears to be actually happening. No way, doctor, I protested, with all due respect. I'm sure it's just a touch of arthritis or something like that. Won't Bengay help? I don't mind smelling old. I know a sobadora who works on my father's bursitis who'll massage all that out.

No, Miss Santos, she insisted. What you are doing right now is called denial of limitations and the sooner you face your degenerating condition the sooner we can develop a treatment program suitable to your symptoms.

Oh no, I said, way low under my breath, muted as the pop of a soap bubble. But the truth was that Saturday night, when returning from work, I couldn't stand up to get off the train, tried twice before a kid reached out to give me a hand.

What happens when you've used up all your good motor units that have been compensating for the defunct ones most of your life is that you end up one day between spring and summer at the disability office. Fortunately for me, I guess, doctors, now knowing that polio could strike the same victim a second time decades after the first vicious attack, no longer write off those suffering from post-polio syndrome as psychologically disturbed or think that all such women are really going through a bad menopause. Unfortunately, the medical professionals have concluded that what I have is genuine and has no cure. No booster shot this time. No intense rehabilitation. The only plan now is to try not to use up the muscle reserve I have left. Needless to say, in view of the rigorous profession I chose, my reserve is almost nonexistent.

Happy fortieth birthday, Carmen.

Since I cannot take public transportation anymore and standing up all day became impossible anyway, the pizza gig is out.

I can't say I'll miss it since the pay is just a few dimes over what I'll collect from being on disability anyway, I tell my best friend Vicky who's about as far away from destitution as I am near it. She was really good at math and is now some kind of executive downtown for a bank. But it does mean I have to say good-bye to my nice preferred physician.

And say hello to days that will drag out waiting to be seen by an endless line of ever-changing interns, Vicky sighs. Just like my brother, she says. You'd think by now the system would be better organized about people with AIDS. Because Vicky's brother Virgil is so sick, I don't see much of her. That plus the fact that Vicky likes making money and spends a lot of time at it.

When we were in our teens Virgil invited his kid sister and me to his Sunday soccer games. He played on a Mexican team, Los Toros or something like that. Every weekend we got to feel like regular girls, sitting on a bench cheering on Vicky's cute, athletic brother. Because Virgil was a star player, we got special treatment from the other team members, too. But I was so infatuated with Virgil I never paid attention to anyone else but him. The infatuation was mutual although he acted a lot cooler about it than I did sometimes. Maybe because he was a hotshot or maybe because I was jailbait. After that first time the three of us never fooled around all together again. But I fooled around with Virgil alone and sometimes just with Vicky. Vicky made love to me like a man and Virgil like a woman, or put another way, I lost my virginity to my best friend Vicky. Then Virgil went to Mexico to play professionally. Vicky went to Princeton. I met Agustín and that was the end of my hermaphrodite romance with the brother and sister.

When Virgil came back to Chicago a year or so ago, he was sick with AIDS. We went out again a couple of times but only as friends. Our affair was long over. But I still remember when he used to whisper to me in the backseat of his car, You're the only girl I'll ever love, Carmen. At the time I didn't really believe him. Later I came to realize that no truer words would ever be spoken to me by a man.

Most of my cuates on the team have died of SIDA, Virgil told me on the first night we went out. We went to a Latino cross-dresser bar called La Luna Llena. The front window was all boarded up from a big brawl the night before. La Luna Llena had gotten itself shut down by the cops a few times because of its "overenthusiastic" crowd. Virgil looked away. He looked away, tapped his fingers on the bar to vintage Donna Summer on the jukebox and sipped on his carbonated water. He didn't drink alcohol anymore but he did chain-smoke. It's a habit I picked up living in Mexico, he said apologetically, everybody smokes there, even the street kids.

You should dress up and perform here sometime! I said, Just

for fun! I knew he was sick. I thought he needed some fun again in his life. Except for his Prince Charles ears he still looked like a Greek god. He blushed. You know I'm not an exhibitionist. I started coughing on a piece of ice from my drink that had gone down too fast. When I recovered I said, First you were the star of your own band, wearing those real tight pants. You remember . . . with the sequins? Then you played professional soccer in little shiny shorts . . . Okay! Okay! Virgil smiled with hands up for me to stop. So maybe I *am* a little bit of an exhibitionist . . . ! And tell me you never shaved your legs, even back then! I teased him. His face turned red as a rutabaga. I know the expression is "a beet" but I like rutabagas better.

Once he started getting sick all the time, we didn't see each other anymore. I called him a few times with no return calls, then silence. I only hear about him now through his sister.

What I like about Vicky the best in recent years is how she never lets me feel how successful she's become compared to me. She gave me a really pretty watch for my birthday. It's got a little diamond that you pull out to set the time. In the end, I say to Vicky, all the interns will say what every joint in my body screams at me now: Jump deck! This ship's gonna blow! Vicky shakes her head and takes a little sad sip from her strawberry margarita. I know, hon', she says, I'm sorry.

Cinco: Period cramps are not like jocks think . . .

Period cramps are not like jocks think, a tightening in the hamstring that with a few push-ups you can just work out. One early morning, just as the neon light of the Hollywood Hotel went out, I woke up with miserable cramps. Miserable. Every month a woman's cycle plagues her exactly the same way for years and years. She hates it. She waits anxiously for it. Relieved to get it, relieved to be over it. Then the day will come like my mother has warned, when it finally goes away and you cry all the time, can't believe you would have ever missed it.

I tried to recall a time when all my mother did was cry and I can't. But there was a long stretch when she yelled a lot. Now I know it was menopause. I'd thought it was my adolescence that was getting to her.

I had a hot water bottle wrapped in a towel on my cramping tummy when Manolo knocked. I knew it was Manolo because by then I knew his knock, soft like the rapping inside my chest. When I opened the door I saw he was carrying two tall café lattes or cafés con leche as he liked to say. Wait! he said. He went to the refrigerator in my kitchen area and filled two glasses with ice cubes. He hummed like a milkman making a delivery, happy to have a job, to be alive at dawn. What was he humming? A song about a woman from Málaga with black pretty eyes beneath those two brows. Brows you can't forget. If she feels disdain for her lover because he is poor, he understands. He doesn't offer riches, he offers his heart. He offers his heart alone. Manolo hummed this, all the while looking at me. As much as I loved that song and wished I had the voice to hit the high notes I wanted to tell him to shut up. Cramps put you in a very bad mood. But despite feeling a little homicidal I just smiled, listened and wondered if anywhere in that long song someone gets killed.

He brought over the iced coffees with a little twirl and swivel of his narrow hips. Here, guapa, he said, handing me a glass. Good-looker, he called me, little dove, my life, my little heart, with such naturalness I would have thought it was his habit to call people by such endearments, like an old calorra grandmother who doesn't even bother to learn people's names anymore. But except for me, I never heard Manolo call anyone by anything but their Christian name.

I sat up and he helped prop up my pillows. When I was comfortable, he said, Drink, mi amor! Go on! Try it! He waited to sip his until I first tasted mine. He was smiling like a boy at nursery school, very pleased with himself that for a change he was doing something for someone else. It was very good, which meant he must've put in a lot of sugar but I tried not to think about the sugar or my cramps anymore and he seemed content just to watch me as I drank while holding his hand, by the fingertips that reached out to my own.

He rubbed my stomach. Poor little one! Little sick one! Maybe we'll be lucky next month . . . , he said, leaning over to kiss me. And then, leaning over some more, he kissed my aching, swollen belly, the careful way you kiss a baby's head, placing his cheek on it afterward, resting there after probably a long wearying night doing who knows what. He looked up at me from underneath brows and lashes more unforgettable than the ones in the song.

That's when I noticed that his shirt was ripped at the shoulder. What happened there? I asked. Ugh, he said, putting a hand over the rip for a second, letting the tear drop again like a dead tongue. Can you believe it? I actually got into a fight with this guy.

A fight? Manolo was not at all aggressive. I'm not a fighter, he said. I think the last time I had a fight I was about this big and afterward my bato beat the crap out of me! He didn't like me getting into trouble. Manolo jumped up and began to act it all out. I was at this little party, not even a party really, a few people that got together last night, with Agustín, it was a going-away party for one of our friends. You remember Silvio, you met him once. So much happened to poor Silvio. His cab was stolen, Manolo said. His wife left him for some guy. She took all his money. He decided to leave. Go back to Spain. Anyway, this guy, big, like this, comes in looking for me. Manolo walked around puffed up for a minute. He said I had taken his woman from him. What woman is that? I asked the guy. I don't have to take women.

That's nice, I said and sipped Manolo's coffee with a little less enthusiasm.

He was mad because his woman is in love with me. I don't even know her. She comes around to see me perform and the only thing that's going on is he's jealous over it. He grabbed me right there. I couldn't believe it! So I had no choice but to hit him. He fell and *pas!* Banged his head on a chair! His friends carried him out. Look at my hand. Manolo showed me his purple fist. It was swollen and cut at the knuckles. Can you believe that anyone would want to fight over a *woman?*

I blinked. I don't know, I said. I'd like to think you'd fight over *me.*

Manolo looked at me and put his drink down. Oh no! And he gave a little snort. He shook out his long uncombed hair and brought it back to tie in a ponytail. I—would *kill* for *you.*

Seis: *What's the difference between* flamingos *and let's say . . . the tango?*

What's the difference between *flamingos* and let's say . . . the tango? a petite pale customer asks me when I tell her I used to dance flamenco. Her head's back over the basin and I am shampooing her hair shade number forty-seven with golden highlights. Vicky got this Saturday gig for me as a shampoo girl at Chez Diva's on Oak Street. Vicky is a good friend of the owner's and a regular Saturday customer. She's always getting something done, tint, cut, manicure, pedicure, wax this, wax that. It isn't easy being a diva in the corporate world, Vicky says.

Or cheap if you ask me.

I don't know anything about shampooing hair! I said when she told me her friend said she could use me on the weekends since her regular shampoo girl is going on maternity leave. You got hair, don't you? You wash it, don't you? Vicky snapped as if she were at a board meeting instead of having coffee in my kitchen with me feeling a little more beaten-down than usual. Yeah, I said, although I think I'm going bald. It's obviously stress. The more I worry about having no income, the more I lose my hair.

No you're not! Vicky snaps again. Snap, snap like a Venus flytrap, my friend Vicky goes. She sinks her fingers in and runs them through my hair. It looks like you're growing a whole new crop in there! she says. It feels kinda creepy.

I push her hand away and run my fingers over my scalp too. She's right. I *am* growing in a whole new crop of hair and it does feel a little creepy but nice too. It's about an inch high all around, like newly mowed grass. All right already! I say, giving in to my friend's attempt to find some kind of employment for me that I am qualified to do.

Vicky is sitting nearby with a fat copy of *Vogue* while her hair gets conditioned inside a plastic bag when the customer whose hair I'm washing asks me about the difference between flamenco and tango. I saw how she looked at me from the corner of her eye, with a mixture of pity and embarrassment about my braced leg. Does that bother you? she asked softly when she sat down in front of me. Does what bother me? I said. Then she started asking questions about my life. Maybe she expected me to say that my last job was at the Goodwill so I told her right away that I was a flamenco dancer. I'm not really familiar with "Spanish" dances, she said. What's the difference between *flamingos* and let's say . . . the tango? Ah! I just love watching the tango! she says and blushes.

Well, for one thing, I tell her, in *flamenco* you don't necessarily need a partner. Whereas with tango . . . You know, like the saying goes, it takes two to tango? She stares at me. I start again, You know . . . like the difference between a blonde and a brunette. They both get their hearts broken but for different reasons. She still stares at me but she is smiling a little like a preschooler who really wants to understand something but her teacher doesn't know how to get through to kids.

I finish the shampoo and wrap her head of wispy wet hair in a nice towel, warm and fluffy since we aim to please at Chez Diva's. Let me show you, I say, and I see Vicky look up and smile a little nervously. The owner, who's working on a cut and has never seen me dance, looks up too. The only thing I have learned myself in the last two Saturdays working in the salon is that hairdressers are about the hardest-working people in America and unless you own the business you don't get paid much more than if you were waiting tables.

Shampoo girls make even less. I'm only going to stick around until the end of the month because I don't want Vicky to catch too much slack for having a friend who's an ungrateful slouch.

With the customer still watching my every move I stop and put my hands together. They say dance is all feeling but anything to be really good requires a little thinking first. So I'm thinking. From way far in the back of my head I hear one of my favorite soleares—Qué afortuná soy. "How Lucky I Am," it's called. I look around. Beautiful women, a beautiful Saturday afternoon, why not dance? Why not sing? And I start to move at first a little slowly, like the hand gadget on a Ouija board starts to move mysteriously, causing awe until it suddenly goes wild on the board spelling out its message from the other world. I move away from the sinks and the driers to a little clear space, ever aware that a beauty parlor may not be the best place for any kind of dancing, thought-out or not, but it's as good an audience as I'll get these days. No one can hear the guitar I hear but I start to sing . . . Sale el sol cuando es de día . . . para mi sale de noche . . . hasta el sol va en contra mía . . .

I don't think most of the customers have a clue what I'm say-ing. Actually I don't think they have a clue about what I'm up to at all as my arms go up and my voice gets louder. Live entertainment featured while you get your hair done is anybody's best guess. A few look over at the owner but when she doesn't stop me or treat me like I have forgotten to take my medication they settle comfortably into their seats to enjoy the show. Of course my good leg does most of the work but a solear doesn't ask for much footwork. Y sentí es-calofrío cuando pusiste tus labios flamenco sobre los míos . . . And then in English I repeat it in a spontaneous translation because under those improvised circumstances I really need my audience with me. Agustín as my teacher never seemed to care if our gaje public understood anything but I suddenly feel a great yearning to have each woman in that room know that flamenco is about how women love and are loved. Like the tango. Like all dances. Even if the dance was born in the streets, born of men who had no use for women. Because in the end—who are we kidding? That's all any-body wants. A little love. *Ay! And I felt a chill when you put your flamenco lips on mine!* I sing. I am doing more singing and palmas than dancing these days, and I gathered my long skirt around me, revealing tennis socks, my scruffy cross-trainers. Most definitely the wrong shoes for flamenco. All you can hear on the linoleum is a muffled sound and little squeak of rubber. I am suddenly aware of being once again on the very fine line I have always walked—something between very pathetic and excruciatingly sublime. *And I don't complain to my star* . . . I sing. *So lucky I am* . . . *I do not complain!*

¡Olé! bursts out Vicky when I end my mini-act, her eyes getting a little watery because it's been a long time since she last saw me dance, or maybe because she doesn't complain about her aches and pains either and dances her own dance every day in her own world. Surprisingly Bianca, the owner, puts her scissors down and starts to clap, beaming like a mother, and her customer with her hair wrapped in cellophane enthusiastically claps too. Bravo, honey! Bianca says instead of You're fired, you nut. Fabulous! Fabulous! Gene the other stylist with a pierced tongue says, She's just so great, isn't she? I'm flushed as the other women applaud too and we are all laughing with tears in our eyes, everyone, I don't know why, just feeling good and lucky that the sun comes out in the day for us and not at night like the woman in love in my song.

Siete: Every day at noon, she has started to manage . . .

Every day at noon, she has started to manage the phones for her Guatemalan receptionist friend at the dentist's office two blocks down. All she says—in Spanish—is, The doctor is busy, call back in an hour, but it seems to work for the dentist. Even after her hospital stay, my mother just has endless reserve. I can't believe that she gets ready every day, runs a comb through her hair, puts on a little lipstick and goes to *work* as she calls it, but she does. Dr. Montevideo, whose clients are all Spanish-speaking, gives my mother ten dollars cash and free checkups although not really free treatments. When she had an abscessed tooth not too long ago she was sent to an oral surgeon because of the precautions involved with diabetes. Amá has no dental insurance and the family got together and paid the bill.

The ten dollars is usually spent by the time she gets home. She buys deep-fried pupusas from the new Salvadoran diner next to the clinic or nopalitos at the Mexican supermercado on the way home. We don't live in a bona-fide Latin American neighborhood but plenty of Latinos live here mixed in with the rest because we're all over town now. It's the great Hispanic panic takeover that you read about everywhere. Don't be surprised if we show up in Hong Kong as the new cheap labor there, Abel says.

My mother does her bit for the household and I want to do mine. So after I quit my shampoo-girl stint I take up Abel on his restaurateur-on-wheels offer and go out with his elote cart on Saturday. Be careful, hija, are my apá's last words when he leaves me on a bus-stop bench on a boulevard, the elote cart filled with steaming corn on the cob. Saturdays are my brother's busy newsstand day. He says this is a good corner for business. Regular customers. I'll pick you up at three o'clock, Apá says. I have my lonche in a bag. Inside a secret compartment in the cart I find the latest edition of *The Economist*. I flip through it. I don't know how I got talked into being an elotera for a day but I could use the money.

Is that clean? my first customer asks me. He's got the meanest five o'clock shadow I've ever seen close up and it's only 11 A.M. In a thick Middle Eastern accent he says, I hear the mayonnaise you guys use is spoiled. I don't want to get food poisoning. In Mexico eloteros use a special cream but it is either hard to come by or too expensive to be imported so we use mayo instead, mayo with—just to add that special cholesterol touch—grated cheese.

The customer's wife is covered from head to toe in black. She has nice kohl-rimmed eyes. I smile at her. I don't know if she smiles back. The mayonnaise is good, I tell the husband. I prepared it this morning myself under my mother's supervision. You speak good English, the man says, holding up two fingers. I prepare two elotes for him. Thanks I say, so do you. Thank you, he says. I went to university in London. I'm a trained accountant. But I can't get a job here, he says. I know what you mean, I tell him. He gives his wife her corn and after he pays me he shakes my hand. Good luck, lady, he says.

Two or three more customers stop by before two kids about fifteen or sixteen years old appear out of nowhere and stand next to me. I roll up the magazine like it's going to help. I have some pepper spray in my purse but I'm not going to take my purse out. My lucky nail file is in my pocket but it's two against one. I look around. Way down on another street is a squad car in traffic. He won't hear me. There's nobody at the bus stop and no bus coming. Say bitch, one says. Where's your money? He's standing right over me. Don't call me bitch, I say, reaching into the compartment to take out my brother's money box. The other guy laughs a little at his friend. Fuck you, the friend tells me, grabbing the box. He opens it. There's a grand total of eighteen bucks. Some change. Here goes my life, I think. Killed for eighteen dollars. He puts the money in his pocket and throws the box down. Fuck you, he says again and they walk away, don't even run just walk like street cops patrolling their beat. They stop and look in a shop window, keep walking. They both laugh a little, turn around, look back at me. Bitch, one of them says and they keep walking.

chapter six

Uno: Amá and I spent the summer
sewing bells on . . .

Amá and I spent the summer sewing bells on to Christmas acrylic sweaters. On the bright side of things, it may have helped improve my hand-eye coordination now that my lower limb capacity is slipping away faster than a winter day. But Amá, who has always said work is work, had to admit finally that nothing could justify doing *that* work for such atrocious pay.

The bell gig started with her worrying over our medical bills and her Guatemalan receptionist friend telling my mother about a

Korean wholesaler who needed women to do some sewing for his fall fashion line. Amá is a so-so seamstress but she can get the job done. She's handier with a knitting needle and the receptionist told Amá that that was exactly what the guy was looking for, *girls* who could work with yarn. It was hard to see seventy-year-old Amá as a girl for any kind of work not to mention that at age forty I was no debutante myself. And what did *working with yarn* mean, anyway?

It was light, easy labor, her friend insisted. All we had to do was add the finishing touches, a few last stitches y ya. A nice reason to get out of the house—practically like joining a sewing circle. The *we* part had come about without anyone asking me. Amá just came home one afternoon from her one-hour-a-day employment and said *we* were going to take a walk to see this chino about a job. Amá, like most Mexicans, refers to all Asians as chinos. She knew he was Korean.

The Korean's store was on a busy strip of wholesale shops just like it. One has tons of sports clothes, another purses and all-size bags, another women's wear and hats. African Americans come all the way from the South Side to get in on the good deals. Spanish-speaking and Middle Eastern customers buy wholesale for the Sunday flea markets. The shop was stocked with thrifty, glittery apparel, lots of things in metallic gold and silver. I kind of liked some of it, the fake coin belts, the sheer Dance of the Seven Veils scarves. All affordable. We're not here to buy, Amá said, and I followed her upstairs past the EMPLOYEES ONLY sign.

But nothing I'd ever read before in my brother's magazines or heard on public radio prepared me for what I was hit with on the second floor. It was like something I had studied in school about the Industrial Age, a page right out of Dickens. But this is the brink of the twenty-first century, I thought. And this isn't a book, it's my life. My life in Chicago—not Juárez, where I'd heard these low-tech, low-skilled, low-paying operations existed, but right down the street from where we live. I stepped back and Amá reached out and grabbed hold of me as if I had gotten dizzy from the climb up and had just lost my balance, and was not trying to get out of there like I wanted.

I rubbed my eyes. But when I looked again the woman sweating over the hot press in the back was still there, a puff of searing steam hitting her face each time she closed down on a garment. I saw teenage girls too, about fifty of them with piles of endless acrylic yarn before them, somber and subdued. These weren't British waifs or Jewish immigrants like in my schoolbooks either but chinas and indias—meaning they could be women from anywhere—reedy and dark, thin-limbed younger copies of myself, sewing in mausoleum silence, quick-fingered and agile-eyed, like indentured servants toiling in exchange for their freedom. I thought, You can't do this to people, you just can't! Slavery was abolished a long time ago. Wasn't it?

The place smelled of something rancid. Probably the girls' spirits. Something in me went putrid too deep inside me at that moment. I don't like this place, I whispered to my little mother who, because she had fed us and clothed us by working on assembly lines, did not seem as horrified by the scene as I was. She didn't respond but she did look a little distressed. Are you okay? I whispered. She put her hand over her heart. Yeah, I'm okay, she said in English. Hearing my mother speak to me in English for the first time startled me and I realized it was her work language.

The first thing the boss told me was that I probably was not going to work out because of my disability which he simply pointed to, and since it had taken me so much time to get up the stairs I should plan on arriving a half hour earlier from now on. Amá was of the opinion that the exercise would be good for me and told him as much.

Sit down there, he said, and sent Amá to another table like we were little kids who needed to be separated in order to do our work. ¿Qué tal? I said in greeting to the young woman on the right of me and noticed immediately by the way she didn't respond but looked at me sideways that talking was not allowed. But soon after I started sewing, when the wholesaler took away my cassette player and earphones, saying that the music would slow me down and cause me to do bad work, I was ready to go home.

It wasn't even lunch time.

Amá, whom he had said was way too old and could not possibly keep up with the quotas he set for his workers, was sent home with me. You'd better go back, my mother advised after we got there, a trip that took up most of the thirty minutes allotted for lunch. Amá had worked for almost fifty years burra hard without complaint during Chicago's factory heyday, making auto parts during peace time and hand grenades during wars, undeclared as they might have been, and she sent me back to the front for the next three days until the immigration raid.

I wish I could say that it was me who called them but it was Vicky, my old school chum, successful businesswoman with a conscience and all-around advocate for the downtrodden in her spare time. Vicky missed her calling as a public defender. She always has some wrong to right in society despite the fact that she's so good at making money. Your mother can't keep sending you out to do that kind of work! Vicky said when I told her about the place. We didn't want the workers to be sent off to detention centers or deported but we also didn't want to see such abuse continue. So three days later, when five men and two women rush in scaring the wits out of every-body, the chinos too, and especially the poor workers, I am the only one who remains seated. I have my passport with me.

One of the INS guys comes over and looks a little surprised when I hand it to him. You never know, I say, and he nods, Yeah you never know. He studies the passport and then me. Why are you working in a place like this? he asks. His combed-back hair put a little too much emphasis on his receding hairline in my opinion although we can't help what we've inherited. He's a compact model of a man with a nice smile. He's also pocho like me, shouting orders in a long-lost Spanish the way my brothers speak it.

Overall the encounter is uncomfortably familiar, something I didn't expect, not imagining la migra to remind me of someone I might see at a relative's wedding, but like some sort of heartless robot or pod person. I'm also not sure I should like anyone who works for Immigration anyway, since they disappeared my friend Julio César from Guanajuato who'd worked at El Burrito Grande with me. But then who am I to judge a person's career choice? Work is work, isn't it? My mother would probably like this guy as a son-in-law. Steady job and all.

If Vicky were here she'd remind me that Julio César is not the point, is it? The point here is what is going to happen to all those women who are being carted out right now, a little shaky but maybe relieved too that the inevitable finally happened, but they're in for something now for sure, a trip south on a one-way bus ticket, if they're lucky. If not, it will be an indefinite stay in a detention center. What is going to happen to their children? Who will tell their husbands and their mothers? How will anyone find them?

I nod in the direction of my crutches leaning against a wall. He looks under the table at my outstretched legs, the one in metal armor, the other clean-shaven, sun-tanned in cutoffs. He nods and hands me back the passport. I hope this doesn't sound weird or anything, he says, but you're very attractive. I was wondering maybe sometime you'd like to go out for lunch or something. You like noodles?

I look down for a moment at what had almost been my quota, but if there were any justice in this world it would be collected as evidence of crimes against female labor. I don't want him to think I'm desperate for a date or anything by answering too quickly. I'm undecided anyway. What with this pod Immigration Officer image fixed in my brain whenever I look away from him and his nice smile. But some men make it easy to say no. Guys who think of themselves as men of the world, well-informed and even fun for having developed a palate for peanut sauce. I mean, I can't imagine you get out much, being handicapped and all, he says.

I'm so used to it I barely wince. I smile instead and say, Oh but I do! I go out dancing every weekend, the Club Tropicana, the Casino Royale! I have a few regular partners, great on the dance floor! I size him up or rather down, then go on, making sure he sees me eyeing his soft gut. Although it doesn't look like *you* get out much yourself. Too bad!

· · ·

I don't know if the Koreans work as hard as Mexicans, but they do seem to have a knack for the free enterprise system. Me, I haven't had a profitable idea in my life nor would I recognize it if I did. But according to Vicky, who's about to start the Victoria Lomas and Associates Financial Group, it's only business for you when you have equity. If you find yourself at the other end, you *are* the business.

A week after the raid I was safely back home, prepared to take a permanent disability vacation when Amá's friend and Amá struck up a deal with the wholesaler, who was back in business in no time with a whole new harvest of workers. Amá's friend would bring us bags of sweaters and we would work at home getting paid by the garment instead of by the hour. We'd sew on bells to Rudolph's or Santa's nose, repack the bags and Amá's friend would pick them up. A great plan.

At first ten cents a nose-bell didn't seem too bad. We were obviously not going to get rich at that rate, Amá said and she was right, but all she wanted was to make a few extra dollars to keep up with our bills. Since in her opinion I no longer wanted to find a job and because it was close to but not impossible for her to do so, she thought that working at home was really an ideal arrangement. We could watch television, take breaks to go to the bathroom whenever we needed, eat a hot meal at no extra expense. All the things we obviously would not have been able to do had we gone into the shop.

But one hundred bell-noses later, we were only ten dollars ahead. Can't you sew a little faster, Amá complained. No, I said.

When I couldn't take any longer Amá's telenovelas about tantalizing thin-nose beauties with stick-on nails and their cavalier Euro-Latin lovers who are always kept from each other through some transparent misunderstanding until the end when they invariably get together, live happily ever after and bear the next generation of blue-eyed soap opera stars, I'd go to sew in my room. She didn't like it when I did that because the next step for me would be to take a nap, which I did.

I had a mind to write an outraged letter to someone somewhere about the unimaginable conditions those women were working under back at the sweatshop, but motivated as I was to not let

Amá down again and being no Emma Goldman, I just kept up with the Christmas sweaters. Until one day Amá said, Enough.

By this time it was September and the wholesaler was working on his spring line, which meant sewing on ruffles to collars and sleeves on simulated-chiffon blouses. We only have one sewing machine between us, Amá told her friend by way of an excuse when she asked if we wanted the work. Why should I tell her you don't know how to sew and that my eyesight isn't good enough to sit at a sewing machine all day? Amá said to me after her friend left. The man will think we're just lazy and won't even consider us next time.

Dos: The coldest winter I've ever spent was . . .

The coldest winter I've ever spent was a summer in San Francisco. I think it was Mark Twain who said that, or maybe it was Woody Allen. Obviously neither of them was ever in Chicago in January. The only time that I've ever gone away in winter was when I went with Manolo to San Francisco, where it wasn't winter in January at all, although when it turned chilly every day exactly at four in the afternoon the chill went right down to the bone. The weather in the City, as they call it there, was like a Cubist painting so if you stood on one plane you might find yourself suddenly in chiaroscuro with a swirling wind pushing you toward a warm patch of sun.

I know about the Cubists from when sitting with art anytime you wanted at the Art Institute was always free. When I was in my last year at the School for the Handicapped, just before graduation, I used to go almost every weekend. Other girls my age went shopping or snuck around with boyfriends. Not me. I had no money and no guy ever took a serious look at me. In winter I spent my Sundays in museums. Sometimes Vicky came along or our school chum Alberto. If we had more than bus fare we'd treat ourselves to a sandwich in the cafeteria and pretend we were rich kids from the suburbs. One day I'm gonna be a great artist, I'd tell Vicky although I didn't know how to paint. I'll be your investor, she'd say. Alberto wouldn't say anything of course because he couldn't talk.

When we graduated from the School for the Handicapped Alberto went back to Puerto Rico. He studied at another special school there and became a teacher for deaf-mutes like he had been mistaken for. Now and then I get a postcard from Alberto in his Caribbean home. At Christmas time he sends me a picture of himself with his wife and two children.

San Francisco was a honeymoon or at least the closest thing to a honeymoon that I've ever had. Of course we didn't have much money for fancy excursions but we liked the sunsets by the ocean the best. Manolo would buy two splits of sparkling wine and we'd each drink out of our own little bottle, watching the sun go down behind the rumbling waves of the Pacific. I had never seen the ocean before. I had never had champagne before either. There were a lot of firsts with Manolo despite the fact that he was so much younger than me. It was just like Chichi said about first loves. Whenever they come they hit you hard for life.

Another thing we liked to do was lounge around in the old Victorian parlor in the railroad flat in Haight-Ashbury where we were staying. His friends would drop in and out like sixties hippies, with nothing to do but talk. But the talk was not about government conspiracies. The men spent a lot of time whispering, passing money back and forth, and the women were always up in my face asking me personal questions, sneaking glances at Manolo, laughing wide-mouthed laughs when I'd catch them at it. Manolo was always so cool. What's the matter, bella? he'd ask, putting his hand through my hair with that blameless look that comes from unforgivably good looks. When night fell, if we didn't go out everything would turn into a party.

There was a lot of selling going on too among everybody to make ends meet, mostly of cheap and useless merchandise. Hilda read the Tarot cards on the street every day using a milk carton with a scarf thrown over. Dancaïre sold key chains with pictures of the Zodiac and phony gold chains. Manolo strummed a guitar and put a hat out for change. Myself, I learned to make love beads to earn us a little money. Whether I was a gypsy or a hippie or both or neither, I only knew I was happy and sad at the same time as long as Manolo and I were together. I wanted San Francisco to last like a day without end, to see a sunset wrap itself around the world and for us to go to sleep together and never wake up, but that was just me being what I had become with Manolo, a woman in love.

Mati, one of the women staying in the same apartment, taught me the art of jewelry making. I made earrings, unisex bracelets, necklaces out of small pieces of yellow glass, black onyx, tiger's eye, even real turquoise and jade, although they were tiny bits and altogether not worth all that much. On a couple of Sundays, Manolo's friends took me to a bazaar in Berkeley. His friend Aldo was going around taking orders for pot-and-pan sets that had a lifetime nonstick warranty from a company in Two Rivers, Wisconsin, while his wife Natalia sold scented water in small blue vials. Among the Rastas and their homemade incense and oils and middle-age burnouts peddling lots of junk, and with early Carlos Santana always blasting in the background somewhere with someone trying to follow on congas, we laid out a serape and sold our wares.

Is there anything you don't know how to do? Manolo asked me once as I put a string of lapis lazuli love beads around his neck. The littlest things I did seemed to impress him. Yeah, cook, I said. Don't ever ask me to cook. He stared at me for a moment. I didn't know what he was thinking. You never know with some men and food, but in Manolo's case I just never knew what he was thinking. Then he said, That's fine, *I* should learn. After all, there has to be at least one thing that I do better than you. How will our children respect me if there isn't? And that night he made his first tortilla española. He made it from the memory of all the potato omelettes he'd eaten in Spain. Too much garlic. But garlic is good for you.

The man you love cooking for you is good for you too.

Manolo had been invited to perform around the Bay Area for a month-long gig by some old contacts who needed a male dancer of Manolo's caliber, and he had asked me to come along. Like the idea of having a baby, we didn't think about what we'd tell people, we just went. On that trip I got a glimpse of the splendor Manolo had experienced through his travels. He had traveled everywhere while I had never left Chicago before then. Except for my grandmother's funeral in Texas when I was a girl, but all that involved was two days of stranger-relatives and my first visit to a cemetery with the smell of carnations permanently imprinted on my brain. Carnations always make me think of death. I have to go back to work, my father said despite family protests, and we all returned home to Chicago.

With a city like Chicago what else do I ever need to see, I used to think. We have everything here, I'd say. Just come, Manolo said. So I did and I tasted salt water for the first time, cold as ice, and insisted on stepping into the ocean anyway, although Manolo had to help me over the shelly sand. I saw blue and yellow and hot pink houses in the distance that sprinkled the hills like gum drops and it seemed like you could reach out and grab a handful to eat. Palm trees and sea gulls for the first time too. It's like being in another country, I said.

It *was* another country, Manolo said. It was Mexico, didn't you know? How can you read so much and not know? I don't like history, I said. He frowned then. Not because of Mexico's loss. His people were living at that moment in a non-country, far away, he said. At least he thought that they were still living.

Don't make me beg, Manolo said to me one night at the night club in San Francisco between sets. But I liked it when he begged. He wanted me to dance on stage. We hadn't rehearsed in a while and I felt a little out of shape. Being in my mid-thirties and in poor health, I was seeing myself as going into early-semi-retirement. I would dance only if I absolutely had to; I'd made that clear to Manolo many times. There were a couple of very nice young female dancers in the ensemble. Dance with Lola or Maria or whatever the hell their names are! I said and took a gulp of brandy. Agh! was all Manolo said whenever he got mad.

Manolo went to talk to the musicians at the end of the bar, leaving his drink half finished on his side of the table and me staring at an empty chair. I looked over at him and they all were looking back at me. Then one came over. Carmen! Carmencita! he said, giving me a little kiss on each cheek. I smiled too as if I didn't know that he was on a mission. He sat down and took Manolo's glass. He laughed a little sheepishly, either because he was on a mission or because he had drunk up Manolo's wine, and then he asked, Why don't you dance with us? What's the matter? You can't be tired! You've been sitting down all night! Are you worried about the other dancers? Those girls? Forget about them! We'll give them the next number off, okay? Clear the stage just for you!

Okay, okay! I said finally. I took a look at myself. I was wearing a plain long black dress. It would work fine but I didn't have my shoes. Manolo has your shoes, the guitarist told me. I shook my head. Too much, I thought. Will you call Manolío over here please? I asked. When Manolo came over he didn't look mad anymore because he was going to get his way. He always got his way. Give me this one pleasure, Carmen! Manolo whispered next to my ear. Let's dance just this once together in this place so they will remember Manolo and Carmen forever. All right? Is that asking so much?

When the set began a little while later I was sitting up on stage. The guitarist began to play a malagueña while Manolo and I warmed up with palmas. *I carry you in my heart* went the song although no one was singing it. Manolo smiled at me and got up first. In my simple dress, my hair twisted around in a little bun but with no combs, no spit curls, no flower over my ear, I'm sure I looked more like a widow than any idea the public may have had of a flamenco performer. Even though I had taken off my brace to dance it wasn't too hard to see something was off with me from the first step I took. What was I doing up there anyway? I could feel the audience asking itself, not saying it, of course, they were too polite, too politically correct like they could only be in the Bay Area, but I could feel it just the same. At the second verse, *You are my only love,* I began to sing to myself mostly under my breath as if in a dream, which corny or not was how everything I did with Manolo felt. I moved toward him, standing just as straight as he was, waiting for me.

From another fountain I won't drink, he whispered back. The resistance from the audience changed to an excited stir as our magic began, two brujos casting spells on each other. I lifted my dress ever so slightly. Manolo had even polished my worn shoes, knowing I would say yes that night, and after I looked down I glanced up at my lover and we smiled at each other. I put a toe forward. Click, come here, said one heel, and then the heel that always lagged behind repeated the command. Manolo came toward me. Just when I could almost feel his breath on my face we both spun away from each other, not just once or twice but even a third time in perfect synchronicity.

Now the stir around the room turned to crackling embers. Manolo removed his hat and put it on my head as we danced and I pulled off my shawl and threw it around him, pulling him close then letting him go. He laughed, yanked the shawl and used it as a jump rope, once in the air like a grasshopper and then he put it back around my hips and pulled me toward him. *In my heart I take you . . . you are my only love . . . and tho' far from you I am . . . from another fountain I won't drink, though I die of thirst . . . !* The cantaor sang the brief verse on his feet. All the while Manolo and I didn't take our eyes off of each other. His look told me what to do next, how to move toward him or away, when to stay in one place and follow him with palmas. It was a short number and our performance ended quickly, Manolo's sweat sprinkling everyone on stage like holy water. I sweat too, but since I didn't spin like Manolo it just ran down my face and inside my dress, following the law of gravity, like everything else about me was doing by then in my life. He ended on one knee and drew me upon him as the audience applauded and cheered and seemed happy to see for themselves that Carmen la Coja indeed danced for all she was worth.

To dance as we did together that night Manolo had to slow down just enough for me while I worked double-time. This was how we were on stage, everything coming easy to him and me working twice as hard. But with everything else, Manolo said, it was always the other way around. Everything else about us that came without a hassle to me, to live in one place, to make love in the same bed every night, to talk it out when you aren't sure what you are feeling or what the other is thinking, was next to impossible for the young gypsy who came into my life one night, almost by accident, and very soon left the same way.

.   .   .

When I returned from the City by the Bay, happy as a new bride, complete with an album of photos and a tea set painted with silver dragons from Chinatown even though I don't like tea, word reached me that Agustín was pretty upset about my suspicious disappearance.

Another word that also got back to me was that he was living with his swan maiden, la Courtney, who was now the star of his company.

But I didn't care. I was zip-locked into my new lover's heart. I didn't want to think about Agustín anymore. There was a part of me that was indebted to him and always would be, of course, the part that belonged to the music. But while no other flamenco maestro could have seen what Agustín had once seen in me, now he was no longer seeing it in me.

So I hear you went to California, he said, when he caught up with me at the Hollywood Hotel.

I hear you have a new roommate, I replied.

Don't believe everything you hear. Then he grinned.

You lying dog, I said.

Agustín made a little sound under his breath. And what kind of dog have you been lying with? he asked.

Ask Courtney, I said.

I'm asking you.

I got up and hobbled over to the window. Sometimes he made me so tired I couldn't walk at all, couldn't even look at him anymore much less speak to him.

You'll regret this, Agustín warned.

But I didn't.

I don't regret anything.

Tres: *Where are you off to, beautiful Jewess?*

Where are you off to, beautiful Jewess? That's the first line of "La Petenera," my favorite song of all time. La Petenera the beautiful Jewess was from Petenna de la Ribera, a town in Cádiz in the south of Spain, according to Agustín who taught it to me. It's played with a siguiriya binary rhythm, only backward, an old Sephardic tune and the first song I learned to dance to with Agustín. It has countless lyrics, countless versions sung over countless years. But it's not as old as the stories that the lyrics borrow from, and still the song, like the story, grows—a Darwinesque song that transforms and survives everything, from great faiths to odious suspicions.

La Petenera was a rich and lovely heiress unable to marry because of her Semitic faith in a time when Catholic Spaniards had reconquered the country with a vengeance. She would have had to renounce her religion if anyone found out about it. *I'm on my way to find Rebeco in the synagogue,* she sings. But what happened with "Rebeco," whoever he was, nobody knows because a rejected lover killed her.

Most gypsies don't even like to perform it anymore, Agustín told me when he first played it for me. Why is that? I asked. It's such a beautiful song! Yeah, he said, but it's bad luck. Or at least that's been the feeling in recent times. The first woman who ever danced it in a show died on stage.

Oh, I said. Later on, Agustín said, the next woman who danced it professionally received a telegram right after the performance. Her brother had died.

Oh, I said, again. But how could a song bring bad luck, I thought. Still, it took a while before I decided to perform "La Petenera" in public and when I did it was with Manolo. Obviously I didn't die. But Manolo left me not long after.

Maybe it *was* a bad luck song. The French writer Prosper Mérimée stole the story of the Jewess, Agustín said, and took it back to his country. Whoever heard of a gypsy woman leaving her camp to work in a factory in the nineteenth century? Agustín said. In the story of the cigar-making seductress, she's called Carmen because Carmen means enchantress, witch. I'm Carmen too, but I'm sure that's not why my parents gave me that name.

Mérimée's Carmen becomes a Spanish gypsy, a gypsy being more exotic and sexy to the French than a nice Jewish girl. That was also Agustín's theory. Women who are sexy are always pagan, that's *my* theory. Pagan too is another song, a Mexican one with verse after verse that my amá taught me about the weeping woman. An Indian man sings to "la llorona." He has watched the weeping woman come out of the temple one day, lovely in her heavenly blue huipil, an Indian-style dress. He yearns for his unrequited love to be returned but doesn't think he's good enough for her because he is a lowly Indian. Everyone calls me the black one, he says, black but loving. That was five hundred years after La Petenera was killed by an admirer. Carmen in the nineteenth century is killed by her jealous gajo lover. Death and desirable women are a big theme in music and in life too. *Don't love me so much,* another Mexican song goes. I thought of it a lot back when Selena the pretty Texan performer was shot and killed by the president of her fan club.

CAN YOU LOWER THAT? Amá shouts from the living room where she's watching TV. I'm singing loudly along with Maria Callas on my cassette player in my room because of the way she pours out *Madame Butterfly.* I think that Maria Callas also must have suffered for her beauty and forbidden passions. WHAT'S GOING ON IN THERE! Amá shouts again. I lower the volume, but it's not the same so low. Still, I go back in my mind, meditating on women ridden with unfulfilled yearning, the wingless gruesome sirens screeching their own sea arias, punished by Aphrodite for not loving gods or men and still men can't resist them. Odysseus had himself tied to the mast of his ship to resist their noonday song calling him to join them at the bottom of the ocean. Mérimée. Bizet. Agustín. Manolo. Sometimes, I'm telling you, it's just too much and I can't sleep at all.

All of these lyrics and recurrent murderous nightmares welled up inside me the night Agustín said he was coming over after our last show. I said I had a headache, that I thought I was starting my period and I wanted to be alone. The truth was that Manolo and I planned to meet later. It doesn't matter, Agustín insisted. I want to be with you.

Just as I was about to tell Manolo not to come over I stopped myself. Aphrodite's anger had caused me to nest among men's skeletons beneath the sea and frankly I was tired of it. My two lovers were not gods or real men. They just thought they were. And if Manolo, whenever he did become a man, was to deserve my love, he was going to have to show me. I'll see you later, I whispered to him as I gathered up my things. Yes, preciosa, he whispered back and gave me quick pecks on each cold-cream-clean cheek. Agustín was smoking a cigarette at the door and took me by the elbow as we went out. I looked over my shoulder to see if Manolo had noticed, but he wasn't in sight.

It was about 4 A.M., with me lying wide awake in the black stillness of my room, the clock tick-ticking like a time bomb, Agustín snoring next to me, when I heard the tap-tap of Manolo's familiar knock. Tap-tap simple as rain and still I didn't move. If I got up I might wake Agustín. If I stayed in bed he would eventually hear the knock that was getting a little more impatient each time. Tap-tap, pas-pas, until finally Agustín stirred. Answer the door, Agustín said all of a sudden, his voice clear like glass so that I knew at that instant that he had not been sleeping at all but perhaps had been waiting like me. What are you waiting for? he asked as I hesitated, stuck to my side of the bed.

You answer, I finally said. I surprised myself at the defiance in my voice. It's your house, he said. But if you don't, I will. Still, I did not move. Answer the door for your lover, he said finally, and I sat up and turned on the light. Why don't you answer, I asked again, crossing my arms over my bare breasts. If you don't answer I will, he said again. Go ahead I'm waiting, I said.

And then he looked at me in a way that he had never looked at me before. His eyebrows going every which way and something furious stirring in his eyes. It was an unsettling look, but even though I stared right back I didn't know what it meant. Meanwhile the knocking had stopped. Finally Agustín, still in his shorts and shirtless, got up and went to the door and flung it open with a *whoosh!* No one there. I thought that what I had seen in Agustín's eyes was fear, fear of a confrontation where no matter how it ended, three hearts would be broken. The look he had given me before getting up stayed with me a long time. It gave me a little bit of susto. *Susto* means the willies.

I'm going downstairs to get Apá's tequila, I tell Amá, remembering Agustín's eyes. Want a shot? All right she says. She seems a little bewildered by my offer but still she won't say no to a nightcap tequila. What life-loving woman would?

Cuatro: The devil is not always as black as he is painted.

The devil is not always as black as he is painted. Agustín liked to say that to me when we first got together. Not because he was fair-skinned and was speaking about himself, devil that he was in my life, but because I looked so sweet and yet he had never known a woman who always did as she pleased. No matter what you say, Carmen, he always told me, I know you don't belong to me. Not now not ever. So I was the devil, in other words a woman who would never surrender herself.

The devil is not always as black as he is painted! he said again one evening when he didn't even bother to knock, just pushed the door open. That was before I got the double-bolt lock and it was the reason why I got it afterward. You always know what to do afterward.

Just a few nights after he first tried to catch Manolo coming over to my place, he burst in like a narc. I jumped. Then I composed myself quickly in order not to give him the upper hand. When the door flew open I thought it was a drug addict breaking in again, but no, it was Agustín. I should have known, I said, trying not to let on that he was scaring me a little with all his dramatics. Were you expecting me? he asked, and I could tell he had been drinking. Is that why you're alone?

I said nothing and Agustín, who had never raised his voice to me, whom I had never seen raise his hand or fist to anyone ever, was making me shiver because I did not know what he was capable of after that big entrance. Just as I was thinking that, I heard everything on my bookshelf, the knickknacks, telephone answering machine, cassette tapes, wind-up clock, go flying against the wall. He reached for the hanging posters of all our shows next and then our pictures in their frames and when he was done with all that my plates and glasses became flying missiles breaking into smithereens. Meanwhile I did not move but sat by the window shivering.

It was a long way down from the seventh floor so I was hoping that Agustín would get the throwing out of his system before he got close to me. He wasn't saying anything or maybe he did say something, but nothing I could repeat since it was all in Rom and loud and gurgled, and then one of my neighbors pounded on the wall and yelled CUT IT OUT IN THERE so Agustín stopped.

You are going to regret it, Carmen! he said to me from across the room, straightening his hair and his shirt collar trying to recover a little decorum. No, I'm not, I said, still not moving from my chair but still wishing I wasn't so close to the window. He pulled out a chair and took his cigarettes out, automatically offering me one. No thanks, I said.

Chichi stuck her head in. Are you okay, honey? she asked me, ignoring Agustín. Yes, I said and smiled. She looked around shook her head. Uh-huh! And then she left. I could always count on Chichi to be there for me at the Hollywood Hotel. That's why when she was killed just a few months later, I couldn't bear to live there anymore.

I looked around too. What a mess, I said. It's your fault, he said. What if I go to your place and ruin everything? I asked. What will your Courtney say?

Forget about Courtney, Agustín said. And forget Manolo for God's sake, will you, Carmen?

No! I said. No! I said again. I will not forget Manolo. You forget him. Leave us alone.

Get it into your calorra head! he said, pointing to his temple. During intense moments between us, Agustín always insisted that I was really a gypsy, the only kind of woman who could really get under his skin, he said. Manolo is not good for you! he scowled, the veins on his neck popping out.

You are the one who is not good for me, I said. I was no longer shivering but shaking hard. Go away, Agustín! It's over between us! *You* get it into *your* head, for God's sake! Stop making me look like I'm foolish! I'm not!

You are! he insisted. You are and you will see it for yourself. I told you earlier you are going to regret this. Manolo is my godson. He is like my blood. He's calorro. We don't betray each other that way. If we do there's a big price to pay. God help the woman who comes between two brothers!

Oh shut up, Agustín! I said. You are in the twenty-first century.

Agustín stared at me as if he was waiting for me to explain what I meant by twenty-first century. Shut up, I said again, helping myself to a cigarette. I didn't even smoke anymore.

Cinco: What player for the Bulls won six NBA championships?

What player for the Bulls won six NBA championships? I asked Manolío mío when he came over the day after Agustín tore up my studio. He was carrying a bag of groceries. I'm going to make some gazpacho for you! he announced in a rare domestic mood. He looked around. Where're all the bowls?

Come on, Manolo, I said. It's not a trick question! Please do not tell me you don't know who the greatest player in basketball history was! I lit a cigarette and slumped down on a chair. Of course I know, Manolo said. Why are you asking me this? And what happened to all the plates? He looked around as if dazed by the mess. To everything . . . ? He stopped pulling out tomatoes and garlic and onions from the paper sack. Wait a minute . . . When did you start to smoke again? he asked. You know that's not good for you, Carmen! Manolo yanked the cigarette from between my fingers and put it out. There was this whole silent question between us about my not having gotten pregnant, my not-so-great health being our best guess.

I cut my eyes at him and lit another cigarette. For several nights after that near-encounter between my two lovers I had been waiting for Manolo to return. By the time he had I was convinced that they were locked in a time warp and a duel between them seemed inevitable. Take ten paces gentlemen, before you turn around to shoot. A *duel?* In my dreams! But still I gave each one the benefit of the doubt, the chance to stand up for his love for me, to stay.

I know what you're getting at, querida, Manolo said. I know a lot more about what goes on out there than you think. But it just doesn't have anything to do with *us* . . .

Who's *us?* I asked. *The people?* What about me, Manolo? What am *I* to you?

I know there are things you don't understand about calorros or you don't want to believe, Manolo tried to explain. I know I shouldn't have left the other night, but I also know that I shouldn't have come. Until Agustín says things are finished between you, I just can't . . .

But *I* can say things are finished! I protested. I could and I would have ended it with Agustín, but Manolo had asked me not to. He didn't want Agustín to know anything about our plans. I could have just told my lover of seventeen years that I had no love left for him and that was that, but Agustín would not have accepted it. As it was, even with having figured it all out on his own about Manolo and my own apathy toward our relationship lately, he wasn't going to let me go.

Manolo shook his head. He looked around and once again took in that my place was in shambles. What happened here, Carmen? Did someone break in?

I glared at him. Take a guess, Manolo! I give you one guess what happened here! He stared at me for a second and then looked down and with one swish of his arm suddenly tomatoes and onions and garlic and two or three bugs scurrying on the counter went into orbit. I'll be right back! he said, and then he left.

I stared at the door he had slammed behind him feeling just a little more worn out than usual by so much nut-cracking and so few kernels. Between Manolo and Agustín I don't know who had more bluff and bluster. Manolo went off acting angry at Agustín, but I knew he wasn't ready to face him. In the calorro community Agustín was big-big. He wasn't the kind of man you took anything from and furthermore told him you planned on keeping it. Manolo's bato had been bigger, but he was dying. Big for them was not like two CEO guys who find out one day out on the golf course that they're screwing the same administrative assistant. So you fire her on Monday or you both laugh about it over a cigar after the game. Big for my lovers meant you'd better defer to the one with more age or who's proven himself to his people or you risk a lot. Anything could happen to you and nobody would have seen it. An ostracized gypsy, as Agustín had told me many times over the years, is a very damned soul indeed. Manolo may have kept up with Chicago sports, but with everything else he existed in another sphere.

But these were their laws, their lives to live out and die from. And I was always only as alone and on my own as my individualized dancing style, not calorra, just a woman with shattered dishes. I knew Manolo would not come right back like he said. He'd gone off like so many times before to forget everything in a crazy night.

So much for the gazpacho dinner.

I don't know what it is about this place, Carmen dear, Chichi said when she came over to help me clean up again, but everything gets broken, squashed or thrown out the window sooner or later! Please don't rub it in, I said under my breath and then I smashed a tomato hard with my hand and wiped the mess on my blouse. Chichi was so shocked, clearing tomato juice out of her eyes, that her mouth dropped open and for once she had nothing to say.

chapter seven

Uno: There are two occasions that
gajes are never invited to . . .

There are two occasions that gajes are never invited to by the
Rom people: weddings and funerals. So when Manolo's father died it
was a while before I knew about it. Besides not inviting you to attend
the funeral, they don't like you to talk about the dead, name the
dead, evoke the dead. When Manolo finally came to see me again,
we did not mention his father. It was as if the man had never existed.

Manolo was drinking a little more than usual, although he had not ever been much of a drinker. Even sober, there was something remote about him, indifferent. He gambled, threw money at pool games, cards. He'd say he was coming over and then wouldn't. He'd drop by unexpectedly and have an outburst later if he hadn't found me in. He'd accuse me of having another lover although he had no evidence of it. Then he'd beg my forgiveness for his accusations. It just went on like that for weeks—the petty business that occurs between lovers when the radiance of their infatuation for each other dims and it is time to decide if you want to stay or not.

Then one day in early summer, the cloud that followed Manolo's unspoken mourning went away and we were in love again. I know you would never ask, he told me one night, softly in my ear, but I haven't been with another woman since I fell in love with you.

And when exactly was that? I wondered.

When we first kissed, don't you remember? He cupped my chin and shook it as if that would jar my memory. At that party . . . don't tell me you don't remember! I went right over to you . . . you were so beautiful, just standing there alone, you looked a little lost, out of place, and without thinking I went up to you and kissed you . . . and you kissed me back! What? You don't remember when we first fell in love?

Of course I remembered. I remembered the startling kiss, the way the cool night air caressed my face when I ran out afterward. I remembered Chichi coming home that night at about the same time and telling her about it, us giggling like two coeds in a dorm. One night months after that she ran into Manolo in the hall. *Now* I get it, honey! Chichi said, Um, um, um! Anybody looks that fine who would come over and put his lips on my mouth would have me acting like a fool, too!

And when I knew I loved you, Manolo said on another night, loved you from my soul, was when my father died. The moon was cloud-streaked and we had just come back from a long walk. Back in my little room he held me suddenly like I was a hummingbird egg, something absurdly fragile and impossible. Because being in love and loving are different things, aren't they? Manolo asked. I learned that from you, he said. Maybe you didn't know it, but I did. And it scared me to love that much, filled me with anguish. What is that? I would ask myself. What is that that makes me want to drink when I don't want to drink. I dance with women and afterward I lose interest. And the whole thing with Agustín. How can I forget how long you loved him?

I stayed out nights because I couldn't sleep and couldn't stand to be inside just awake and thinking like that. The cock fights with Agustín, the money I lost gambling, that was all a way of forgetting. That's why I didn't come around. When my mother died, my father used to say to me that a part of her lived on in me. That is why I danced the way I danced. I danced for two. But what happened when my father died was that a part of me died with him. Of course. Everyone told me that. Something died like a long winter had killed it forever. And then I remembered you, mi amor. Your face would appear before me out of nowhere and I didn't know which way to run. But I realized then that the reason there was no escaping you was that I was not alone anymore and I knew I will never be alone as long as I love you. As long as I love you. You can stop loving me and maybe one day you will. I wouldn't blame you. I know I've done you harm. I know I wasn't with you when you needed me. I know what I am. But I will never stop loving you—my one root to this earth. Never.

Dos: Here's what I must say now.

Here's what I must say now. Of all the deaths I have lived through, this is the hardest one to recall, the one I don't accept, not without a corpse as proof.

One night when Manolo showed up out of nowhere and I had been waiting again, out of nowhere I heard myself say, I don't want you in my life anymore, Manolo. Water brimmed along Manolo's dark eyes and began to stream down, not solitary tears but a steady thin stream from each eye.

Why did I ever have to know you? he said, barely loud enough to hear, without looking at me, as if he were asking himself and not me, so I didn't answer. So you regret it? I asked instead. It was the closest that Manolo and I ever got to breaking up until then, saying such harsh words, words never having been the best way we talked to each other anyway.

He put his hands on his forehead and covered his eyes like when he had a hangover and every sound made his head throb. I stood up and rested a hand on each hip. I was aware I was looking down at him sitting awkwardly on a foot stool, looking smaller by the minute and me suddenly becoming big and bad like Aphrodite. I didn't like it. I wanted to be emanating something, but not fear. Fear was all the three of us seemed to have left inside anymore, all that we were bringing out in each other. I'm going to call Agustín, I said. The three of us should talk it out in the open once and for all. I'm sick of both of you.

Then what are we going to talk about? Manolo asked, looking up at me. I turned away. Fear and love together are a little blinding.

Manolo and I stayed like that without words for a while, and when he said, Amor mío, each word felt like it weighed a ton. Who are you calling your love? I asked. Don't call me that anymore! And then, without even thinking about it, I said again, I don't want you anymore, do you hear me? I don't want you anymore.

We looked at each other, like a venomous spider was building a web between us so that if either of us moved we would die. Then he went on his knees and softly, like a cushion falling to the floor, he fell forward. His arms circled around my skirts and he cried into them, soaking the pleated satin. Try to understand. Please, amor mío.

What do you want me to understand? I asked. I really wanted to know. Manolo's bato had left him to Agustín, but it wasn't as if Agustín were free to be with me, as if Manolo were stealing away Agustín's ghost-wife in Spain. It was just me. Carmen. The woman who belonged to nobody and everybody at some time or another and in the end only to herself. I had chosen to be only with Manolo, but no one seemed to be interested in my vote, and Manolo was caught between loyalties.

His long curly hair was loose and glistening like seaweed underwater. I ran my fingers through it. What is it? I said again after a while, this time my voice cracking a little. When he seemed calm, but with his face still sopping up my skirt, he said, I can't have you.

I waited for more but that's all he said.

Am I so monstrous to claim? I asked Manolo when he stopped crying, maybe a little too abruptly for me to take his tears to heart in the end. Don't get me wrong. I was moved at the time, but just because a man cries on bended knee, it doesn't mean you have to feel sorry for him. Manolo reached up and pulled me down, yanking my long-sleeved leotard over my shoulders. I had a hard time coming down because I had a brace on, so I settled myself on the stool, damp skirts bubbling up around me like a lily pad.

No, he said. No . . . you made loving you easy and leaving you impossible. And he kissed me hard with closed lips on the mouth. He got up, picked up his coat on the bed and left without saying another word. I sat there for a long time in my lily pad.

I really hated him. Hating Manolo made sense because I loved him, and more importantly he loved me. I noticed my nails and reached for the emery board. Usually at a moment like that I'd reach for a drink but instead I gave myself a little manicure. Manolío would be back, I told myself. He'd leave countless of times and come back countless of times like a newly discovered planet that astronomers were trying to figure out, what it's up to, what to call it, whether it really existed or was just an illusion. And one day he'd come back and stay.

I knew that then and I still know that now.

Tres: I don't like pain, I really don't.

I don't like pain, I really don't. I don't even like talking about it but sometimes it feels better if you complain a little, if you whine, let out a toothache whimper, at least now and then. So I tell my mother one day that I feel just lousy, lousy all the time, even in my sleep and when I wake I feel worse, and then I just look over at her and start crying.

Ever since I began to experience all the pain that I had not felt in so long and never thought I would again because I was strong and smart and young and could dance my way through it, I've been trying to figure out an escape from the little ice box that is my body's ongoing agony.

There are better days, as they say. On those days I get around a little. I celebrate and make espresso. I'll cut up a fish, red snapper or

salmon, for Amá and me and put it in the broiler. I'll add two pota-
toes and make a little butter-lemon sauce, although she will be the
one who has to finish up the task because by then some part of me is
hurting too much.

Vicky or some other single friend—for some reason it's only
single friends who take time to visit lonely women like ourselves,
women without the obligations of children or activities with partners—might come over with a video. What else should I bring? the
friend will ask cheerfully on the phone, and we'll spend the whole
time talking while it's playing because I'm not so interested in movies anymore now that I miss my life.

I begin to sob out of nowhere, as I said. I sob right there in the
living room while Amá doesn't say anything, doesn't even stir. She'll
surely reproach me for this sign of weakness sooner or later, but I'm
too deep in wallowing to go back now. Save your tears for when your
mother dies! she used to yell at me when I was a kid and upset about
something and wailing in my room. My amá taught me a long time
ago that tears will get you nothing and nowhere and as far as I know
she was right.

I'm propped up on the couch with one of her acrylic afghans
thrown over me, and she's sitting in her favorite chair. We had been
watching a young Barbara Stanwyck on the American Movie Clas-
sics channel. Amá put the remote control on mute, but she's still
staring at the screen. Some elasticized minutes have passed with
only the sounds of my weeping and then I see her heavy lidded black
eyes with the reddened whites brim with tears that she would rather
not spill, not for a daughter who's about to give up, not for the skinny
girl who fought for her life and grew up and became an uncontrolla-
ble woman doing whatever it was she felt like doing, which to her
family looked like just one big Hungarian folk festival. Amá cannot

waste her tears on that. She wants me to get up and walk, drive her to the grocery store. Go out and find a husband, have children, one or a dozen. Carmen, you love to read so much, why not become a writer? You don't need to move around for that! She's suggested that I write children's books; they say there's money in that. Be a famous writer like that Mexican woman who wrote the novel about food! What a beautiful movie! she says, imagine eating roses! Everybody likes to eat! Write a recipe book! You don't have to do much exercise to accomplish that, she says, and after all the books you've read you must know how to write one.

I stop my wailing when I hear Amá first sob. I've never seen her cry, never, only a small sob at her mother's funeral in Texas just as the casket was being lowered into the ground. Even then she covered her face with both hands so that I didn't actually see her. I figured that's what she was doing because her body quivered, like a little electric shock had just gone through her. And then she stopped.

She stops now too, and pulls out a crumpled tissue from her apron pocket to blow her nose. Ay, hija, she says after she's composed. You have to be strong or you won't get better. ¡Ay, hija! she repeats. You don't know—if I could have taken away your suffering, I would've. You don't know how many times I have thought that, how many times over the years. She sighs a long, heavy, mournful sigh, tucks away her tissue in her apron somewhere and picks up the remote control again.

Cuatro: It was our last gig before . . .

It was our last gig before summer, when Agustín customarily left for Spain for the season. My participation in the show had already been reduced to one brief solo number and to sitting out the rest of the program, doing palmas, calling out olés at appropriate places and looking pretty, if also a little weary, with the rest of the women gathered up on stage like a big bouquet of wilting orchids in a room with no air conditioning.

Manolo had come around again. We should go to Spain, he said one day. We'll start over, have a family. I agreed. We needed to get far away to have a fighting chance together. Despite Manolo's reassurances I noticed that he was discreet about us around others, including Agustín. *I*, myself, didn't even talk to Agustín much anymore at that point. He was pretty involved with Courtney, so things seemed to have worked themselves out on their own, I felt.

Since I was obviously not earning enough from dancing for such a trip I took a part-time job serving refreshments at a small movie theater. My pores sweat artificial butter but I didn't care. It felt right to do whatever had to be done to save enough to be able to leave and start a new life with Manolo. He himself performed in restaurants and bars regularly and traveled around the country doing gigs. When he was back in town sometimes Manolo surprised me at the door of the cinema when I got off work. This is how it was with us, surprises and besitos and I just didn't worry about anything. Although I wouldn't take money from a man for my needs or my wants, whenever he couldn't come himself he'd insist on giving me cab fare from work. He didn't want me to walk so much or for anything to happen to a woman with a brace making her way around in the city at night, although I'd tell him that is what I'd done all my life. Not with him, he said.

I was worried myself about Manolo that evening when he didn't show up at the gig, but when Agustín didn't seem bothered about him having gone AWOL on us I knew he knew what Manolo was up to. That was the way they were with each other, acahuetes, as my mother likes to call them, pals who are partners in crime. *Acahuetes* is not just a Spanish word, it is Mexican, goes back to the Aztecs, my mother says, and I'm sure she's right although I don't know how she knows that.

Agustín would tell me when he was ready, I was sure. Before the night was over, he'd say it, maybe just a hint to torture me because of his ongoing jealousy. I felt sorry for him so I just held my tongue. There was nothing Agustín could do about losing me or about losing Manolo either, I thought. He'd just have to face it.

Instead, Agustín announced that he had to leave for Spain sooner than he planned because this summer his tour was going to begin right away. Good, I thought, good riddance.

That's great, someone said, for you and Manolo!

I don't remember who it was that set off the alarm in my head without realizing it, just said what he knew. He surely must've meant that Manolo was indeed going to perform with Agustín at some point in Spain, I told myself. But not that he was going *with* Agustín because he and *I* were going together, not right away but when we had enough money. Agustín would have nothing to do with *our* trip. Manolo and I talked about that.

He's still in big demand, that kid! Agustín said. We've got a lot of requests to perform. I wouldn't take the gigs without him and he said he wouldn't take any without me—a package deal is what we told everybody! Take it or leave it! This time Agustín looked at me, just for a second.

As soon as I got out of the club that night I went to find Manolo, but not right away, not looking frantic. I wouldn't give Agustín the satisfaction. When I was ready, costumes and makeup packed, I made my way for the first time ever to the apartment Manolo was staying at, but where I had never gone to before because he was a man who didn't like questions, and keeping away from a man's home is the best way to avoid asking them. I was told he wasn't there. I went home and called every fifteen minutes and still no Manolo.

Sometime late in the night my confidence started to crumble and I called Agustín but got no answer there either. I called his number and then Manolo's and never once found either one the whole night. It went on like that the rest of the weekend. You just missed them, I was told everywhere I asked. When will they be back, do you know? No, no one knew anything. Asking someone else about your lovers' whereabouts was already a bad sign.

Finally I caught up to Manolo one night in one of his favorite bars playing pool. He didn't even know I was there until I was right up behind him and turned him around just as he was about to shoot. Oye Manolo, one of the other guys said, a young calorro with a goatee. This must be Carmen. Yeah, Manolo said, looking embarrassed. A woman I hadn't even noticed before sauntered over from the bar. Who are you? she asked me. Haven't you heard? I asked her. Soy Carmen. Never mind, Manolo told her before she could answer. He took me by the elbow to lead me out of the bar.

I had never been in that place although I had known about it because Agustín had always told me it was a snake pit where he and Manolo went to gamble. Who was that snake? I asked Manolo when we got outside and were alone. He wouldn't look at me, while I on the other hand kept searching his face like a roadmap to tell me where we were. I looked at his face but he avoided my eyes. Never mind, he said to me and lit a cigarette. I slapped it out of his hand. We were both startled at my anger. Manolo—is it true that you are leaving for Spain with Agustín? Is that your choice—that man over me—or what? I was so outraged I wanted to bawl my eyes out. But like when I first got polio and got teased by regular kids for just being myself, I didn't cry. I shut my eyes tight-tight until the urge went away.

Of course I am not choosing Agustín, he said. But he still wouldn't look at me. ¡Mírame! I yelled, and as I did I saw a few of the calorros come out of the bar just to watch the show, including the snake.

Carmen please, Manolo said. Agustín and I—we're family. Don't you understand that? How can I forget the past between you two? He has feelings for you . . .

I wanted to just walk away. But like so many times in my life, ashamed to have anyone watch my awkward walk, I just stood there. Maybe I should have realized that what was so shameful was the awkward situation I had placed myself in that night. Finally Manolo looked right at me. He looked as if to say, Okay? Can I go now?

I turned away from him and stared at the stop where I would have to wait for the bus home. It seemed a lot farther away than when I had gotten off. Hey Manolo! one of the guys called. You still playin' or what? The snake laughed out loud and went inside. I watched Manolo turn around slowly and go back in without another word.

Manolo always had the best walk.

Cinco: *During my desert hermit*
days . . .

During my desert hermit days I found in an old church a
painting of San Sebastián bearing such an uncanny resemblance to
my lost beloved that I started going to Mass. I even went to confes-
sion. I just wanted to talk to someone about Manolo. One Saturday I
got the priest to come out of the confessional so that I could show
him how much Manolo looked like San Sebastián, the way his eyes
searched the sky in agony. My boyfriend had that look too, see? I
said to the priest. I said boyfriend because I really didn't know how
to refer to Manolo's place in my life, although "boyfriend" when
you're past a certain age can't help but make you sound silly no
matter what. The priest studied the photo I took out of my bag and
then the painting. Hija mía, he said finally, scratching his balding
head, maybe you should find someone, get married. There are
women who shouldn't be alone so long. It's not good for them.

I miss Manolo so I still see him everywhere. What are you
staring at? Amá asked me the other day when I was holding up one
of my oblong tortillas that I had just taken off the griddle. I could
swear that Manolo's profile was burned on it. My mother was eyeing
me in the way that priest had looked at me, with pity. That's when it
came to mind that maybe what I have felt for Manolo all these years
isn't love at all but a very unhealthy fixation. (*Obsessed* is probably
more accurate but I feel a little better if I just say *fixated.*)

To further investigate that questionably objective glimpse into
myself I made an appointment with the therapist I had seen a few
years ago, the one who sent me to take a ceramics class as an alternative to my life as a dancer. He was obviously not cut out to be a

career counselor, but as far as therapists go how would I really know if he was any good since he's the only one I've ever known? But he practiced at the free clinic so I figured his ear at least was better for talking to than myself.

Mexicans, superstitious as we may be, churchgoers or not, don't customarily place any faith in psychologists. But I had and I would again. Anyway, I'm not really Mexican, I told myself. I looked around like someone was talking over my shoulder. These were the kinds of strange thoughts I was coming up with every day. A major identity crisis. Not just because I'm forty but because I'm forty and falling apart.

Then there are the things healthy people also ask themselves at forty when their career dreams have gone kaput. When they don't even have a job. Well, a lot of healthy Americans don't have jobs, my voice said. Somehow, however, I don't think that most Americans end up doing piecework like my amacita and I did, or find themselves in an illegal sweatshop having to produce a passport or risk deportation. How many Americans fear deportation *out* of the United States? Don't be naive, the voice said or maybe that was Vicky in one of our conversations. I'm not, I said. Yes you are. If you look like a Mexican, walk like a Mexican, talk . . .

I see the shrink only a few times before we both agree that therapy is not what I need. His last advice is, Write down your dreams. I don't dream anymore, I tell him. He stares at me, lights a cigarette and says, Of course you do, everybody dreams. *I* don't, I say. I should know. You do, you just don't remember, he says. I don't see why my therapist would think I would go to therapy to lie but it really bothers me that he's got such a suspicious nature. Smoking's bad for you, I say, waving my hand at the smoke. His office is a little windowless cubicle in the basement floor of a public health clinic.

Outside the door you hear babies crying, workers yelling at every-body, TAKE A NUMBER LADY DIDN'T YOU HEAR YOUR NAME CALLED CAN ANYBODY HERE SPEAK PUNJAB? No plush couch to lie down on, no nicely dressed guy in tweed with an Austrian accent and monocle taking notes like you see on TV. Just this: a paper mess everywhere. A hundred forms to fill out each time to make sure he gets reimbursed by the city for seeing me. A picture of his wife and baby on top of a stack of papers on the cold radiator behind him. She's plain but so is he. The baby looks like them.

He takes another drag and says, I know, but with the baby we never get any sleep. I'm a wreck. She doesn't sleep at night, ear aches all the time. My therapist sighs, takes one last drag, then stubs out the cigarette. I need another job, he says. Years ago I use to dream, I say, trying to get back to the point, which I believe is me. Oh yeah? he says. What did you dream about? He looks at his watch and at the clock behind me and taps his pencil on the desk. He's not taking notes. I don't know, I say. But they were nice dreams, I know that. I look at my watch too.

I had gone to therapy for several weeks when he said he'd find a support group for me. There was a hospital downtown that was sponsoring one for people with post-polio syndrome. People like me, in other words, a little neurotic but with real health problems. There were actually a few of us living in the same city. A group? I asked at first, But that's not a solution is it? Well, at least you could talk to each other about it, he said. Right, I said. Misery loves company.

Well good luck, he says, as I get up to leave after I've filled out his reimbursement vouchers.

.   .   .

Vicky said she'd go with me to the hospital where the group meets. She has had none of the reoccurrences of polio that I've experienced in recent times, but she does, however, believe she's going blind. Vicky's always been a little paranoid that way. Everything going all right, getting great pay and bonuses, buying a new car each year, a MUPPIE queen and yet out of the blue she'll anticipate the worst. She says a doctor she's been seeing claims he's never heard of blindness related to polio sequelae, but there's no telling what horrors are in store for us and she decides group therapy might not hurt her either. She'll go even if for no other reason than to drive me there.

Until I go blind, she says.

We've been going to our new support group awhile when one night it is up in arms about the extent of desertion that goes on in people's lives. You're not only in denial of your limitations, one know-it-all member told me, but you are also in denial of how much you've been hurt by people's *abandonment* of you.

Like who? I asked. The whole circle laughed, if not out loud then in muffled snickers. At least, I *felt* they were laughing at me. Except for Vicky who rolled her eyes, but I didn't know if it was at the group or at me.

Ms. Know-it-all took it upon herself to review my life. I didn't really like her but I have to admit that she was better than the free shrink at the clinic. She had the kind of common sense that you can't get a license for. Well, let's see, starting backwards from what you've told us so far . . . There were those two gypsy guys you were involved with, she began, holding up two fingers and counting.

Vicky rolled her eyes again and this time I knew it was at me. If she was tired of hearing me try to figure out why the two loves of my life had left without the courtesy of a proper good-bye, she could have told me a long time ago when we were alone.

I think there was your flamenco instructor, my support-group peer continued. Didn't you say something about how she had been your teacher for five years and just took off to Spain without ever even checking up on you to see how you were doing? she asked.

Considering that there were eight of us the know-it-all had impressive powers of recollection. In the two months that Vicky and I had been attending I had let out my laments in snippets during each session, starting with my estrangement from Manolo.

I told everyone about how Manolo and I had had a love for each other that surpassed time, not dwelling on the fact of course that I haven't heard from him for a while. Eventually the whole cast of my marvelous drama was brought in: the villainous Agustín and the arch-villainous Courtney. I reveled in the opportunity to have a new audience. Vicky was always letting out a little cough to hint that enough was enough whenever I got going, but I didn't care. I wanted Manolo back and if the only way I could have him was by conjuring him up in memory I'd take that.

I knew I needed help. That's why I was there.

But as the know-it-all brought up a few other details I'd shared they didn't sound as bittersweet when she played them back, but actually a little embarrassing.

The most serious abandonment as I see it, someone else said, is that by her mother.

My mother?

Let me tell you, one of the men in the group spoke up, *everybody* suffers from abandonment by their mother. It's the very crux of Western civilization as we know it, no big deal . . .

And before I could figure out what he meant by *that* another member started to cry and then nobody wanted to talk about anything anymore.

One night after my group meeting I watch a worm that eats all the male eggs it hatches—or whatever it is that a worm produces. It's on one of the public television nature channels that I watch when Amá's gone to bed and released the remote control to me. Only the females survive. The males grow inside the mother and become her *mates,* fertilizing her from within.

I wonder what kind of stage production that would make if the story of the worm were transformed into a woman. The conflict created by abandonment would be resolved when the leading lady eats all her male children, who, once inside her, become her inescapable lovers.

Maybe I'll bring this up in group next week.

Then again, maybe not.

chapter eight

Uno: I wish I had been given a room
with a view . . .

I wish I had been given a room with a view but the only thing I
can see from my bed is the other wing of the hospital across the
parking lot below. I know there's a park out there somewhere but
maybe the rooms that overlook it are only given to people with insurance policies.

I am here because I came up against what the doctor called
the polio wall. One night it was me, not Amá, who woke up gasping
for breath, not my mother but me who thought she was having a

stroke and wasn't. I don't know if the pressure of keeping up with the bell-noses caused my cardiorespiratory problems but something shut my body down at the end of a long sewing summer and now that I am here, I am told simply to rest.

You get yourself depressed because you don't do anything anymore, Amá told me once again one afternoon, sitting with me knitting a hat for someone for the coming winter. I hope it's not for me. She's using up all the acrylic scraps in every color. She kept them from the chino. Look at me, she said, knitting away. I keep busy all the time. I know that if I stop I'll just get sick.

I'm depressed because I *can't* do anything anymore, I said. I picked up the remote control and started channel surfing until Amá gave me a look that said don't do that anymore.

I used to think that dancing was no good for you, she said after a while. But I've been thinking lately that maybe that's what kept you going. Maybe you need to get back to your dancing, hija. It'll give you spirit again. *Ánimo* is the word she uses in Spanish for spirit, as in animism, as in the soul inherently separate from the body.

I close my eyes.

My spirit is off somewhere dancing. My spirit dances all the time. It's my body—my cuckoo out-of-control body—that doesn't dance anymore.

Dos: Carmen la Coja is back . . .

Carmen la Coja is back, I thought after I got out of the hospital. I threw away the backless blue gown I slept in there and put on something red for bed.

I phoned Vicky. Comadre, I said, come with me to see the show at the Olé Olé Restaurant. We call each other *comadre* although neither of us ever had children to baptize, which is what makes you a comadre. Since our days at the School of the Handicapped being crippled was our holy bond. What with Vicky organizing Virgil's home care, researching alternative treatments and sitting with him, she hardly socializes anymore. Could you stand to see a flamenco production in this town without you in it? she asked. My comadre knows me all too well.

I miss it, is all I said to my comadre, who understands right away. Theoretically we're halfway through our lives. You can have a lot to still look forward to but if you aren't careful a whole lot to miss every day too.

．　．　．

The Olé Olé didn't figure to be authentic, owned as it was by a man rumored to be connected and using his place as a front for drugs. Moreover, it served trendy gringo-gaje-style Tex-Mex (which in Chicago is called Mexican, and is better at home). As for the show, it lacked some sincerity as I expected it to. But that may just be how Agustín taught me to suspect anyone doing flamenco that wasn't first blessed by him. Above all, what bothered me was that all the performers were strangers and none looked over thirty.

Except for one seasoned singer, a very good one in fact, who was introduced as a special guest direct from Granada and who announced that he was celebrating his sixtieth birthday. He sang like the oldest saddest crow in the world—lovely, lovely—which made me remember and remember until I didn't want to remember anything anymore and just leaned back to enjoy his performance.

Almost everyone I knew was gone. My old friends Rocío and José had had a baby and moved to New York. Agustín was living in Cádiz, as far as I knew, and which may as well have been Jupiter as far as I was concerned. To me Spain was a myth anyway. But I nearly choked on a tortilla chip when I saw Courtney come out on stage. No one you couldn't care less about ever goes away. Vicky and I were in the middle of our meal when she surprised us by coming straight over to our table during the break. She kissed us both and sat down. Vicky and I exchanged glances.

Would you like some wine? Courtney asked. Why not? I smiled. She went to order at the bar. About ten minutes later she came back, a bottle in hand and with the cantaor carrying the glasses, and invited him to sit with us. Carmen la Coja was a fabulous dancer, believe it or not—for *years!* she told him. He nodded. Overall he seemed elegant in a pressed black suit, white shirt, open collar, decked out to the gypsy-nines. You danced with Agustín, didn't you? he asked in a thick Andalusian accent.

I nodded. I used to dance, period, I wanted to say. I used to dance and I used to drink and I used to move my wrists. I used to make love. I used to be angry and shout at Agustín as if he were a child and no one ever talked to him like he was a child. I used to betray him every Saturday night with his godson who betrayed me because he returned to Spain with Agustín who had also betrayed me with this gaji girl sitting next to me. Betrayals everywhere and all around. They used to live in a condo paid for by her parents. She once put the screws on me pretty tight and squeezed me out of the show, a show like this one tonight, only infinitely better. But now who cares, what does any of it matter? Yes, is all I said.

El cantaor nodded. And then his eyes widened as if it was all coming together for him in the heavy file of his memory bank. ¡Ojú! he said. You danced also with Manolío! ¡Ay! ¡Manolo! He smiled and shook his head. He's tremendous! Then he turned to Courtney: He left Spain—what happened to him? Vicky and I made eye-contact again. Courtney shrugged her shoulders but it was obvious she knew something. He kept looking at her and so did we. He's here, she said. We all looked around. Well, at least it's what I heard. Maybe it was just gossip, she added. We all stared at her. What? She looked around like we had made her feel guilty about something. You mean you haven't heard from him, Carmen? I stared at her with my best poker face. Although with the mention of Manolo's name I felt my left eye twitch. Still, Courtney knew I wouldn't ask anything, from too much pride.

The singer smiled at me like he'd just remembered something, and directing himself to me he said, But back in Seville we heard about *you*—how you danced despite your bad luck.

No one had ever called my leg bad luck.

He was very proud of you, you know, that Agustín. He made you a legend! He laughed a low throaty laugh and swallowed his glass of vino tinto in one gulp. He turned to la Courtney, What time is the next show?

She told him they had a few minutes left, gave me an elbow and said, Listen to this. Tell her about Agustín's life back home. The singer hesitated. He obviously didn't want to engage in idle talk, but then he made a face as if to say, What could it hurt now? His wife was also a remarkable dancer—they danced together for years, he said.

Courtney gave me a smirk. She knew that no one on this side of the ocean had known that Agustín's wife danced and that when he returned to Spain he went to perform with her. He wasn't herding goats or sheep or picking olives or weaving baskets or whatever it was that was his family's mainstay, being the honorable country husband and son-in-law he always claimed to be.

She heard how good you were on stage with Agustín! She was

very jealous of you, the man remarked. Big surprise, I thought. Since the time of her curse, wishing me dead was more likely.

With all the children, she couldn't really keep up with Agustín's music, traveling everywhere, he continued. Vicky let out a little laugh, but I couldn't bring myself to look over at her. The singer tapped his glass in an unconscious gesture, awaiting a refill. Courtney poured it for him. Then they gave each other a sexy look. I saw her hand go on his knee and I thought, Well, why not?

What children? I asked. I figured he was referring to all the children in their village, the children of their clan, the children of Agustín's extended family.

Their children! el cantaor said.

They had children? I asked quietly.

¡Oju! That woman was pregnant every year! he said, sipping his wine. She was just a girl when she was married to Agustín. That's the custom. And every year she was pregnant. Not all of them survived, though.

How many? Courtney asked. Tell her how many children Agustín and his wife have!

Nine, I think. One pair of twins, he said and winked at Courtney. Anyway, he added, I think it's nine, but it could be more. It was hard to keep up with that family!

He told you his wife couldn't have kids, didn't he? Courtney asked me. I nodded and looked away. I started rubbing my sore wrists and pretended I had lost interest in the conversation. He told me the same thing, Courtney said with an expression of disgust.

¡Ay! ¡Que Agustín! the man sighed. He's terrible, terrible! And then he chuckled because *terrible* for him did not mean terrible at all but something worthy of a man's admiration.

Courtney took his hand, Come on, guapo. It's time for the next show! They got up and after the formality of good-bye kisses around the table he turned to me and whispered, I was enchanted to meet you after all this time. You truly are a legend in my country, you know!

Tres: What doesn't kill me makes me vomit.

What doesn't kill me makes me vomit. Oh, I may still recall every color thread in the brocade of Agustín's "lucky" vest and the nervous way he brushed his bristly eyebrows up before a performance. I know that he likes to smoke and eat at the same time. But when I check my gauge I find I don't feel anything for Agustín. It's run out of gas. *It* being something I had no name for but isn't in my heart anymore. The cantaor's revelation about Agustín's lies sealed the coffin. I think about that sometimes when I prefer to tune out the Spanish tabloid-style television program that comes on when I'm eating with Amá, with features like the one about the boy who was born with hooves in an obscure village in Ecuador or the pet pigs that ate up a weird guy's mother in Miami or the blurry paparazzi video of some unidentified babe who was caught sunbathing in Puerto Escondido with Luis Miguel.

There are an infinite number of things that I know about Agustín that once endeared me to him or that annoyed me about him or that made me feel everything all at once that one can feel for an ex-lover and still remain sane. But now, they are just biographical trivia about Agustín—a man I once knew—up for sale to the highest bidder, but there are no takers.

I'm not surprised.

*Cuatro: I haven't been to a fiesta, had
a good time . . .*

I haven't been to a fiesta, had a good time like at the ones I use to take for granted, laughed hard until my eyes got teary, teased and been flirted with, stolen kisses in the dark, sung and stomped my feet until the wee hours of the morning, in ages. I haven't worn my shiny skirts with the big white dots or the black lace trim. I haven't wrapped my hair tight-tight in a bun at the nape of the neck and carefully arranged spit curls around my powdered face. I haven't donned my old self, the one I pretended to be or perhaps was for most of my life.

So when I got a call from Homero, an old friend from my ensemble days, who had come back to town to give a concert and who didn't need me to dance, he said, Just do palmas, sit and look gorgeous, vale? I said, Of course! Of course!

Vicky said she would buy tickets and come with her sick brother Virgil, who might be up for the outing. Great, I said. I'd seen him only once when he had first come back from Mexico after so many years away. He looked like an early Christian martyr, so pale with his torment. A couple of the members of the support group were excited at the prospect of seeing my comeback, the one sometimes only I knew would happen someday.

The day of the concert Homero, who teaches in Mexico City at *El Instituto de Flamencología*, calls to tell me that his female vocalist has a sore throat and couldn't I sing a few numbers for him? He knows I know most of the music. There were all those after-hours parties when we sang together so he knows I have a voice, the voice I got from my amá but that I never thought was as good as hers, who thought she wasn't very good herself, just liked to belt those boleros out with Lola Beltrán on the radio in the kitchen and whistle like a love-crazed canary to Vicente Fernández, whom she says still makes her feel like a woman.

It's my last show, I figure, ever. Has to be, who else but an old friend would ask such a thing of me? I'm grateful to Homero. I love you, I say, two or three times, for including me in your program although you didn't have to, there are others—surely one of them could . . . ? No, Homero insists, It has to be you. You are as fabulous as ever, I am sure. Everyone knows you here. You'll be great and we'll have fun and afterwards I'll take you out and we'll dance until dawn.

I'd sent three of my costumes to the cleaners because I wasn't sure which I would want to wear, maybe all three, although there was no way I was going to get into the shoes and I wasn't going to dance anyway. But my biggest problem was whether I could manage to sit straight for two hours on stage. I renewed the prescription for my pain medication and decided that the best way to get through all of it was just to concentrate on the music and the verses that Homero needed for me to help him out with, close my eyes and not think of my body, just sing, sing with the confidence with which I used to dance.

Have a good time, Amá said, and I took her casual good-bye as a blessing. Amá has not hit a wall but she's hit something because she's not up for much anymore. She doesn't go out anywhere, not to the Guatemalan dentist, not to sneak out for sweets and hot chiles, nowhere. Apá says he'll stay home with her to keep her out of trouble. He hasn't quite moved in but almost. He still sleeps downstairs, though.

It will be a good time and that's all it is meant to be, my farewell to the one thing I ever did that really mattered, if not to anyone else then to me. One day I'll develop the same hunger for some other thing I'm good at and in case I don't, my brother has mentioned a couple of times lately that he could always use a hand at the newsstand. And in summer you could get a corn pushcart of your own, Abel said. It's not really a bad job, despite the casualties. The eloteros will be unionized by then, he says.

.   .   .

I wish I could say that the excitement of performing again sent my endorphins off the charts and that I didn't feel anything but the thrill of it all, but after three songs I had to get off stage because of the searing pain going down my spine. I watch the rest of the program from behind the curtains, reclining on an old sofa-chair prop from some past production.

Still, while I do sing, making my debut as a soloist, I am partly in nirvana, the kind that all performers reach as the curtain opens, tenors and jugglers and just ordinary everyday off-the-street narcissists who relish when everyone's eyes are on them, watching every movement, hearing every utterance, and they feel oh so good about what they're doing and how they're doing it.

When I finish, first there is silence, the kind of stillness from an audience that you suspect must mean, What a fool you've made of yourself but we're so surprised at your nerve that we can't even bring ourselves to react. But a few tense seconds later it is smothered by rich applause and everyone whistling, calling out bravos, and finally I am glad I got up the nerve to sing instead of opting to stay home another Saturday night watching cable with my mother.

The gang was all there, too. I spotted Agustín's old friend, the virtuoso Tomás de Utrera, with a couple of his young protégés. Not just my friends turned up but the Olé Olé clique too. Afterward at the reception, maybe because of my unexpected triumph, Courtney acted like we are old chums, until I discreetly advise her if she didn't stop trying to soak up some of the attention intended for me I was going to have to hurt her. Then Vicky came over and moved Courtney aside.

Vicky's polio was not half as bad as mine. You don't even know she ever had it until she takes a few steps. What happened to Virgil? I asked Vicky. I was disappointed not to see him again, not to have a chance to talk about old times. But I already knew how bad he was. Virgil just wasn't up for it . . . He sends his love, though, hon', Vicky said. Then she sighed, He's starting to look like an angel.

What do you mean? I asked.

Like he's *dying*, Carmen! she said. Okay, okay, I said.

I looked around and kept looking around. If Manolo, whom nobody had seen dancing in Chicago, was just living here, making a living as a French baker or busboy in a Yuppie restaurant, he'd have to come, wouldn't he? He'd have seen my name in the paper or heard through someone somewhere, and he'd have come. Wouldn't he, Vicky? I asked my best friend who remains my best friend because she doesn't indulge my neuroses. So it wasn't cruelty but simply what I needed when she said, Shut up.

*Cinco: Maybe it is some kind of
pity handout . . .*

Maybe it is some kind of pity handout, I figure when I first get the call. I must have looked worse than I thought. Homero thinks I'm dying and he wants to do something nice, put me in the chorus, throw a few bucks my way, save me from the dreary fate of working at my brother's newsstand. Homero called and offered me a chance to record with him in L.A. *Record?* I repeated.

But maybe he just wants to take me to Disneyland, like one of Jerry Lewis's muscular dystrophy kids who are always asking for your change with those little cans set up at restaurant cashier counters. It reminds me of the time Vicky, Alberto and I cut school to go to Riverview Amusement Park. Riverview was torn down a long time ago, but for us city kids back then it was better than anything. We had been there once on a field trip. This rich old guy paid for it, our teacher told us. We were his favorite charity. There was the Tilt-a-Whirl and the Fun House where you walked right into Aladdin's mouth with its funny mirrors and crooked floors, and prizes none of us won at the shooting gallery. But what got to my friends and me the most was the freak show. Outside there were big cartoonlike posters of what we would see inside if we paid for a glimpse of the Fat Lady, the Half-Man and, saddest of all, the Lobster Boy with claws for hands. Vicky wanted us to go back and free the Lobster Boy. Maybe we could get him into our school, she said.

We didn't have any money of course, so we got the idea to scrounge up a few cans in the garbage in an alley and went around begging until we came up with enough to have a good time. Between the three of us it didn't take long. Although you'd be surprised how ugly some people can be out there who walk around thinking themselves decent and good. On the other hand, others just are decent and good without even thinking it, like the butchers at the Supermercado Jalisco. They took our cans right away. Uh-oh, we thought at first, we're busted, until they threw money in from the register and made everyone in the store put money in too. You'd think we kids had just witnessed Our Lady's apparition. We actually felt a little guilty about our deception after that until Vicky reminded us that we had not lied about anything for that money. Just look at us, she said.

We never did get a chance to rescue the Lobster Boy because Alberto's father, who left work after he got a call from the school and went out looking for us, caught us waiting for the bus way up on Belmont Avenue and drove us home.

Good ol' Homero. I'd love it, I say on the phone when he calls to make the offer. But you know I can't just get up and go to Los Angeles . . . !

I know tha', Homero says. He talks English by dropping end-consonants sometimes, it's a little choppy, but also a little seductive. Funny, I never thought of Homero as sexy in the old days. In the old days he was gangly with his tongue tied up in a knot. But he not only sounds seductive on the telephone now, he looked it too the other night, with his salt-and-pepper hair falling over his eyes as he played guitar on stage and led the group in his white linen shirt buttoned all the way to the top, filled out by shoulders that are anything but gangly.

We're willing to wai', Homero persists. He's starting to sound like he's on the up-and-up. My manager has been ravin' abou' you to the producers since we go' back. *We* insis'. We' like you to do a few solos on the CD. Really, Carmen. I don' know why you waite' so long to sing. Tha's wha' you should have been doin' all along! Tha' Agustín! So typical of him to keep someone back. Or maybe you didn' wanna sing? If it's money you're worrie' abou', my manager has already offer' to represen' you. She'll get a contrac' ready for you if you agree to come. Don' worry! Just take care of yourself . . . and that stupendous voice! ¿Vale?

chapter nine

*Uno: You can't call it cheating when
you cheat on a married man.*

You can't call it cheating when you cheat on a married man. I
told myself that the summer I took as my lover a flamenco aficionado
who hung around the clubs when Agustín went back to Spain and to
his wife, as he did every year. To say that Max, who played a little
guitar but was really a jack-of-all-trades artist, was *my* lover only
means that he was the only lover *I* had during the summer, but
Máximo Madrigal belonged to no woman.

How it got started was when one summer evening—Agustín

had been gone for a few weeks and I'd had maybe one brandy past my limit and had slept alone one night too many—I took Max home with me. And then there was no getting rid of him. Voilà! He'd appear at my door at the Hollywood Hotel. Voilà! He'd be gone again, back and forth making his rounds, and before I knew it the steamy city summer would be over.

If I'd had any money I would have spent my lonely summers in Hawaii but since I didn't and I had to work, Max was as close to "getting away" as a poor girl could manage. He never asked questions or made demands. We just had a little fun and that was it.

Now, after all these years, Max, who heard I was back on stage, calls me to have a drink at his place, his way of saying come over and have sex. I make my way there without much fuss. There's no one to hide our affair from anymore. I dress in a thirties-style crepe dress I had someone copy for me years ago from a vintage one that I found in San Francisco and that fell apart the first time I wore it. I dab a little laurel oil on the back of each ear, on the pulse point between my collar bone, but I don't paint my eyes or rouge my cheeks. If I learned nothing else from my retreat into the desert, the tough love of my support group, the other night back on stage, it is that only superficial beauty fades with time. Like a pearl, the longer you wear it the more sheen it has, that's how a woman of substance begins to show her beauty. That's me. I am not sure what Max will see when he opens the door. But his call alone let me know that at the very least, I am a woman unforgotten.

I see the light on the top floor when I pull up in the cab. His silhouette is at the window. Keep the change, I say to the cab driver. Before I am out of the cab, trying to struggle out gracefully, I feel Max's hand reach for me. Here, permit me, he says. And I do.

. . .

*H*allelujah! says Vicky when she hears about my latest rendezvous with Máximo Madrigal and brings over a bottle of Tres Generaciones Tequila, the good stuff. Let's celebrate, she says, not Max's return, what woman would celebrate that?, but the exit of Manolo's ghost. Like he didn't leave long ago, girl, and it's not like he fell into a black hole like you'd like to think, just face it once and for all, damn it. What you were doing with a guy who carries a switchblade in his back pocket, I don't know. It must've been good with him is all I can fathom! she says, and pours us double shots like a bartender from the Wild West wiping off the little she spilled with her hand, licking her fingers. Manolo carried a switchblade? I ask. It's funny how you forget little things like that when it *was* good, I say, just to get on her nerves. Vicky scrunches her nose. Like you needed Máximo Madrigal, professional puto, to tell you that you are beautiful. I tell you that all the time, but no! Don't listen to your comadre! Vicky just goes on and on until a few rounds later her speech gets slurred and mine too and then we both get a little sloppy and just keep saying, So what? But so what to what, neither of us is sure. Before the night is done with us—or is it the aged tequila—I decide I'll take Homero up on his offer and go to Los Angeles to record. I'm going to be a star, comadre, you know that? I tell Vicky. What? she says. You mean you're not one already?

Dos: I call Amá from Hollywood.

I call Amá from Hollywood. Hi, Amá, I say, Guess what? I'm in Hollywood. Oh, sí? she says. I'm actually in Long Beach, which is where Homero's recording studio is but Amá doesn't know where Long Beach is so I say Hollywood because maybe that way she'll know I'm headed for stardom. But instead she just says, Good, good, hija . . . ! She's distracted, I can tell. Do you need something from here? she asks. Whenever Amá gets a call, it's a bad time. Either she's in the middle of a Spanish soap or she's got a tortilla heating up on the stove and was about to sit down and eat, is what she tells people. She gets upset when her family and friends don't check up on her, but she gets annoyed whenever they do. No, Amá, I say, I just thought I'd let you know how things were going.

They had gone okay considering I'd never recorded before, didn't even know I could really sing until last month. The rest of me doesn't feel so great, though, but Homero traveled with me and that helped a lot and I only had to do one song our first day in the studio. I liked all the new ideas they have come up with for traditional flamenco songs, a mixture of Middle Eastern with a jazz flair to it. What's all this? I asked a musician named Fain when he came in with an array of strange objects. They were his instruments. This is a tar, he said, and this is a guimbris and this, a buzuki. But mostly I play bass, he said. Oh, I said.

The CD is Homero's concept. Homero's a genius, I think. Ees going to appeal to a global music audience, see? he explains. As for me, I like hearing my voice played back with the strange sound effects echoing in the background, all with a little rumba dance beat. His manager Phoebe Browne seems all right too. She produced a contract right away. Don't want any wrong ideas about what we're doing, she said. I remember when I worked for Motown in Detroit in the early days. Those young people, so talented, so naive and so full of themselves always making unrealistic demands! So now, it's all here in print right away! She puts eight pages in front of me. I don't know what I signed. But Homero said it was the same contract he has and he's been fine with it, he says. Really, don' worry!

I signed a contract this morning, I tell Amá but she doesn't sound like she's there. Amá? Can you hear me. Huh? she says. Of course I'm here! You just caught me in the middle of my novela. I look at the clock, figure it out, yeah, it's time for her favorite soap. She watches several throughout the day but this one has got a new hunk actor that she likes, the son of the son of an idol she had a crush on when she was a teenager. My seventy-year-old mother suffers from intergenerational movie-idol worship. Okay, I'll let you go, Amá! I just wanted to make sure you're okay! You feelin' okay? I ask. Yeah, yeah! she says. Your father took me to the doctor today. My blood pressure's fine. The doctor said I'm doing better. We can't afford this call, hija, take care of yourself. Let us know when you're coming home so that your father can go pick you up!

That's okay! Homero's coming back with me, Amá! I say loudly. I don't know why I talk so loud on the phone when I talk long distance to either of my parents. They shout too. They're not deaf. Neither am I. We'll take a cab! Don't worry, I'll see you Sunday after next, okay, Amá? Okay, okay! she says and click, I'm off.

Tres: *I'm still at the Sea Winds Motel, compliments of my new producers . . .*

I'm still at the Sea Winds Motel, compliments of my new producers, sleeping in the next day when I answer the telephone to a gruff tobacco-drenched voice so familiar it could be my own but I'm so knocked out by painkillers I say, *Homero?* I know it's not Homero.

The voice is not harmless like Homero's, which is honest and giving, but loaded instead with carcinogenic treason.

Es Agustín, he announces. It's a sign of some sort, I can feel it right away but not whether it's good or bad. I'm not psychic but I can feel that it means something.

What's the matter? he says when I don't say anything. Were you sleeping? Are you okay? Of course you're okay, he reassures himself. Agustín is one of those people who can carry on a conversation all by himself and won't take it personally at all that you don't contribute. I hear you're recording an album! Is it true? Is Homero pulling my leg or what? How did you manage that? You know you always did know how to get what you wanted!

Hmm, I say. I've outdone him. That's why he's called. What follows next I really can't believe. Ese Manolío! he says. He took off on me too!

Too? I don't answer. It is just like Agustín to shift things around then put them in front of you like a cheap bar trick, to think he can dupe you into believing you didn't see what you saw, didn't feel what you felt. He had left (presumably for his wife) and he took my lover with him and now he's implying that Manolo and I had both abandoned *him!* I should hang up, I thought. But I don't hang up. I'm a coward. He knows it. He knows all my weaknesses.

He thinks.

I'm still quiet so Agustín continues catching me up. Manolo left for Serbia, he says, to find his father's family. I think he was gonna try to get them to Germany. Germany was giving gypsies asylum. Although, he tells me, there was that story about some young gypsies there who came upon a big sign along a fence that said: GYPSIES, GET OUT! One of the kids went to yank the sign down and when he did a bomb went off and blew them all up. Manolo's a good kid, I guess. He's got guts. But he left me in the middle of a gig. Oye, Carmen? Are you still there?

I'm still here, my stomach has just gone sour. It's too early for such a call, especially without coffee. There's no room service at the Sea Winds Motel. Where're you calling from? I ask drowsily. I'm back in Chicago! he says, like it's good news. I just got back . . . ! Agustín keeps talking and pretends to be glad about my new recording contract. But I know him better. As my mentor, he really believes he is the one who should have the big break. Finally one of us is going to crossover to gaje society! he says. Now they'll know what good gypsy music is! By the way, do you guys got a good violin player? You know you need a good violin player . . . Agustín is not asking to get in on the deal himself some way, at least not yet.

There should be more between us, I think but don't say out loud, after having been together for so many years, more than just a one-way conversation about my success. He taught me everything he'll brag and in some ways he'll be right. Although he also often said that flamenco, like poetry, is not something you can be taught. But I don't say much, just listen and not even that really, when suddenly Agustín stops and then says, What? Are you still mad about Manolo? What were you going to do with a twenty-year-old anyway?

I could have handled *twenty* twenty-year-olds! I blurt out like a fire hose. You're darn right I'm still mad about Manolo! Unless you pay her rent, who a single woman sleeps with is not your business, I said. Or like my mother always said, Carmen, you do not have a stepfather. No man besides your father has a right to tell you anything. So what right did you ever have to interfere with my feelings for a young man? What I didn't want anymore was one old man!

Old man! Agustín sounds amused but I know he isn't. Not only a twenty-year-old but a gypsy! he says. What did you expect from him, Carmen, devotion?

Then silence again. Agustín with nothing left to say. It's weird. And then he says it because it wouldn't be Agustín if he didn't: Gitana, he calls me, you don't know how much I've missed you, sabes? What do you think? His voice is real low, like he doesn't want anyone to know what he's about to admit. I mean . . . is there a chance that we could try again?

After a few long seconds I say, Yes . . . Agustín. There's always a second chance for anything to get started up again. And then I add: But weren't all the years *we* spent together enough?

That's what I thought, he says and hangs up. For a long time I hold the telephone to my ear hearing the dead line until a cold recording comes on and says, If you think you've dialed the wrong number please hang up and try again.

Cuatro: *What do I need feet for when I have wings?*

What do I need feet for when I have wings? I think one night as the digital clock slowly counts off the hours and I can't sleep for wondering whether or not I am really a singer now that I am not going to dance anymore. Isn't that what Frida Kahlo wrote somewhere in a journal or on a painting and made everybody see how brave and wondrous she was?

Easy for her to say, she was a painter, not a dancer.

I won't be remembered like Kahlo. I know. I was never wondrous. Not like María Benítez either, living flamenco legend who

had her own dance company and whom people flock to every summer to see in Santa Fe like she was the open-air opera incarnate in
her silk costumes with dolman sleeves, her long arms all over the
place and an expression on her face when she moves across the floor
as awesome as the goddess Kali's. I don't even come close. But like
Kahlo, Benítez, Kali, I'm not afraid. No matter what you do, when
you are first a woman it means you cannot ever be afraid.

Cinco: Why are you called Carmen la Coja?

Why are you called Carmen la Coja? A young woman asks me
at a chain music store where I am signing my new CD. My manager
Phoebe Browne is with me. So is Homero who seems to enjoy referring to me now as his discovery. We're in New York. Chicago was
first, then Los Angeles, New York and finally we'll go to Washington,
D.C.

I'm on the cover in the red satin dress I bought in the garment
district in L.A. Like my mother I can sniff out a bargain a mile away.
In the shot, the group is around me, all of us already looking famous.
Because I used to dance I answer my new fan—one of countless
now, it seems, that appeared with my new CD. I'm sitting at a
signing table and wearing a long dress. She can't see my braced leg.
She stares at my picture on the CD and then at me. She doesn't get
it. *Coja* means cripple, I say. I'm beaming like a hundred-watt light
bulb. There's very little lately that can get to me.

I returned to Chicago with my first payment in hand. That was
ten months ago. Amá got a little teary-eyed at the sight of the check,
evidence that for once my musician friends were not really scam
artists, and that instead I might just have a little talent after all. She

gets it all from her old man, Apá said as always. Wouldn't you like to think so, my mother said. Abel asked if I wanted to invest in business with him and I said no. We're going shopping for once, Vicky said. And no offense Carmen, but I don't mean to Wal-Mart either. Things were quiet again after that until the CD showed up special delivery one day at home. Everybody kept passing it around holding it so carefully and staring a long time like the Holy Grail had just been mailed to our house. Amá took out her magnifying glass and studied the picture to make sure it was really me. Nobody, starting with me, could believe that I was really officially a singer.

And now here we are, on tour.

Why would someone call you that—a cripple? the fan persists.

What exactly happened to make me a bit of an overnight celebrity I don't know, but suddenly to others I'm a fantasy come true, a Colombian emerald, Dorothy's ruby slippers skipping down the Yellow Brick Road. Yeah sure, it's reflected a little in the upgrade of my costumes and in my new haircut. People always associate a little fame with fortune whether it's true or not. But just like that the pity is wiped away from their gaze and in its place is a wish to be you. I've been seeing it since we've been on our concert tour. One day I'll go back to Kansas, I'm sure, I say to Phoebe and Homero over pasta pesto and Chianti one night in L.A. But I'll enjoy it while it lasts! Are you kidding? Phoebe says, you're just beginning, kiddo! Homero laughs, ¡Ay, Carmen! I'm so glad I discover' you!

I'm not a continent, I said.

Yes! I know tha'! Homero says with a reassuring smile.

Because I *am* crippled, I tell the fan. She shakes her head as if I have offended her. You shouldn't say that about yourself!

Maybe it's a cultural misunderstanding, I say. In my culture people get called by their most evident characteristic. I really am a *coja!*—so it's okay! Lifting up my dress, I put out my bum leg and she takes a peek around the signing table. She really looks bewildered since it isn't clear what culture I'm talking about. We're listed under Latin and International and World and Pop/Reggae. Although I'm not sure why, we're even under Musicals. It won't help clarify things if I say I'm from Chicago. She shakes her head. I think she's going to cry. Never mind! I say. I can't dance anymore so now I'm singing! The young woman tries to cheer up. That's good, she says. She looks at the guy standing in line behind her. He grins as if he couldn't care less if I can walk or not and just wants her to move aside.

In each city we give a concert and in each city I spend most of my time in my room before and after performances. I order room service. I rent movies. I take pain pills. When it's finally time to go home I have to say I don't-won't-couldn't possibly miss life on the road.

The biggest change however is in Amá. Big surprise, the respect that money will get you even from your own mother. With each bit of cash I am able to hand over to her she relaxes just a little more. She even told Apá to get a new family car. Maybe she won't drive it but he could drive us, she said. Let hija do what she wants with her money, Apá says. She's earned it. And what? my mother asks. What about the bills? The roof needs repair! You know that! And the pavement outside! You want somebody to fall on that big crack and sue us? Amá goes on that way, shuffling around the house, pretending to be dusting, keeping busy. My father smiles at me as if to say, Don't mind her, which of course I don't because the truth is I can't remember my mother being this content in years.

Apá is only being polite, too. He knows they could use the money. It's not as if I've made a fortune so far anyway, just enough to make a slight difference, enough to make Joseph and his wife come over and be nice to me, but not enough for them to invite me over to their house. So, do you get to drive around in a limousine? my sister-in-law asks. She's told all her friends at work about me, she says. I took your CD and showed everybody! And your brother too, don't think he's not bragging to the guys at his job, too, that *you're* his kid sister! Every time your song comes on the Smooth Jazz radio station that they play all day, he says, That's my sister! Joseph doesn't look very pleased that his wife is telling me this, since he's always been the success story of the family. But finally he relents, Yeah. And then adds, Maybe you'll be able to help out the folks now with your new fortune!

I ain't got no fortune! I tell him, trying to keep things light. But my sister-in-law's smile fades. She's obviously disillusioned. Yeah, yeah, yeah, Joseph says. I know you people in the music business make a ton of money when you get a hit on the radio! Ya! Amá says to us both, meaning cut it out.

Negrito comes over one evening again and no one in the family even says anything about it because he is my guest. I take him out that night with Vicky and Virgil. Vicky and I keep up the conversation over drinks, pretending that both Virgil and my brother Negrito don't seem like they are vying to be Jean Genet look-alikes—tortured sensitive artists with self-destructive underground vibes. Virgil's chiseled face has been stripped to bone and sores. He's a Lazarus among the living. At first I'm a little horrified since I haven't seen him in so long and then I get used to it. And my own brother weighs less than I do.

So . . . you don't play soccer anymore at all, huh man? Negrito asks Virgil, who is still sweet but hardly has much to say and now shakes his head. The whole night goes like that. Obviously our brothers don't fit into a lifestyle of cloth napkins and wine lists as long as your arm. But then neither do I, I think. I don't know when Vicky made the leap over to the other side of the fence where she is so confident, without a bit of pretension, but I'm guessing it was about the time she got accepted by the Ivy League.

We should go hear some blues tonight, I suggest, or some jazz. Who's in town anyway? Everyone smiles politely but it's pretty clear that the excursion is a flop. We're all still too young to be so sick, so burned out! I sigh. No one responds; too burned out, I guess. The waiter recognizes me and asks for an autograph. My, my! My sister the celebrity! Negrito says. I've never heard him be sarcastic with me. Sure he can be as biting as the next Chicagoan but not toward me, not until then. Your sister *is* a celebrity now, Negrito, Vicky says quickly. You and your family should all be very proud of her. Then she turns to her own brother. Virgil, if you're tired we can go home. Virgil closes his eyes and I swear I think he is not going to ever open them up again and then he does. When he does we are staring at each other and he smiles. Remember Carmen? he whispers. I nod. Me too, he says and smiles. Now I see what Vicky means by Virgil looking like an angel and when he shuts his eyes again, I feel he is tumbling down down down from heaven. When he lands I have held out my wide long skirt to catch him and like on a trampoline he bounces off and goes straight up to the sky again.

Seis: Every week in group I take out the paring knife.

Every week in group I take out the paring knife. I peel away and peel away and I suspect that finally there will be nothing, like what my old yoga instructor told me happens when you are in pursuit of the meaning of life. Ultimately you find that existence is nothing, the void. But to achieve the void is everything, the very essence of existence. This void, to me, is what happened in pursuit of love. I'll leave the meaning of life to those who read Greek or Latin or take trips to Tibet.

I went to the desert to live like a hermit in search of her soul, I tell my group members. People say that hermits are in search of God but when you get that far away all you find there is yourself. In the desert I heard the strangest sounds at night. I slept alone, I ate alone. And one day I decided enough was enough with the desert and returned to the city.

I returned to the city with its traffic honks, the hollering noises, its rush-rush of people, made a little money selling ties at the mall out of a wheelless wagon when the invitation to dance in Germany came. I had never been to Europe. (The group likes this part, even Vicky, since it's hard for most of us to travel.) I thought that being on the same continent as Manolo I might hear his heart beat again. The exile to the desert had not cured me of my nostalgia for my lost love. But all I heard in Germany was the rumbling of trains going back and forth and laments for their own wars, their great lamentable wars, and no one but no one noticed the little ache way in the pit of my stomach, way in the pit of my empty self. There were too many broken hearts in Germany to hear mine, which went clink clink like porcelain as I walked and when I danced. The last time I danced.

So how does it feel to be famous? a new member of the group asks. I really don't feel fam— I start to say. How should she feel about it? someone interrupts before I finish. Sometimes I think it would really help if we had someone in our group to keep us in line, like Amá, for example. I heard your song on the radio the other day! another guy says. Pretty good stuff! Congratulations. What station is that? I asked. I have never heard my music on the radio. I know the CD is selling but I really can't say how it all happens. And I don't feel famous no matter how many people say it. The new gospel program, the guy says. You know the station . . . right after the Howard Stern Show? Howard Stern? I say. Never heard of him.

Siete: Guess what? I saw Manolo . . .

Guess what? I saw Manolo, Abel says to me one day when we run into each other in the backyard. He's putting his elote cart into the garage for the night. He cleans it out and scrubs it down and the next morning bright and early he gets his corn-on-wheels going all over again. I'm sitting with my parents having a beer. I've been so busy lately between Phoebe's calls and plans for another CD and maybe another concert. Vicky got me on a good insurance plan now that I can afford it. What's next is she's talking me into buying a condo in her building.

My parents never knew Manolo so my brother's announcement means nothing to them but to me the planet has just stopped spinning. My hands grip onto the arms of the lawn chair I'm sitting in. I don't say anything.

Abel goes into the house and comes back out with a beer. He sits down. I still don't say anything. It's a nice clear day, an extraordinarily ordinary day. I have just been enjoying the afternoon with my parents, taking in some sun. We're talking about the new car they bought this past weekend. Life is good. Life is not Manolo anymore.

Manolo is Manolo in my dreams and in my therapy support group. He's even in the Tarot readings that I have now and then. A young man will enter in your life but he will cause you great pain. Too late.

But Manolo is not real. He is memory and ethereal. I'm staring at Abel just the way Macho stares when the dog doesn't understand what you're saying to it, with a little tilt of the head. There couldn't be a more unlikely messenger than my blubbery antisocial brother. If I buy you a membership for a gym, I ask him, will you go?

No, he says. Then he takes a long sip from the can before he says it again: *Manolo.* Manolo says hi.

It's too much, I think. He's like Edgar Cayce making announcements for the dead. He didn't even know Manolo, no one in my family did, they hardly knew *me* back then. What are you talking about, I finally ask him. Where did you see this guy you claim said hi to me?

You don't have to get hostile, Abel says. He came by and bought an elote asked for lots of chile on it too. While he ate it we got to talking. He said he used to dance with you and he heard you are doing really great now. Yeah, I said, she is. Who would have ever thought Carmen had it in her?

Go to hell, I say. I don't know why I'm so mad at my brother, but I understand now how the tradition of killing the messenger started. I have waited and waited so long and made up so many stories, so many scenes where one day my great love was going to show up and sweep me off my feet again and here he comes along on an everyday afternoon and buys an elote from my useless brother and says, Tell Carmen hi.

Carmen! my amá says. You shouldn't talk to your older brother that way . . .

Yeah! Abel says and laughs. Go to hell, I say again but I don't look at Amá. What do you mean he says hi just like that! That's impossible! That guy's gone . . . he's in Serbia or Germany or someplace in California for all *I* know, but not here, not on the corner three blocks away eating *elotes* for Chris' sake . . . !

Well, Courtney had told me he was back, but who could believe *her* about anything? And while I had scanned the streets theaters clubs everyplace since then hoping wishing thinking but not believing one day my eyes would fall upon him I couldn't believe he would not have come to see me if he were in town. I feel so utterly disappointed. All I know is that it feels worse than the sweat on my skin from the humidity, nasty and slimy. Worst of all, I still want him.

Really broke your heart, huh girl? Abel laughs.

I get up, trying not to let them see me shaking shaking with rage or with joy or maybe desire pouring forth like a genie out of a bottle when the stopper's been pulled out. I don't know how Manolo had that effect on me back then and I don't know why he should have it on me now, but I have worked way too hard and come way too far to have anyone do that to me and get away with it. Nobody breaks my heart! I say, picking up my crutch and waving it at Abel. Hey! he says. Watch it Carmen! Apá says. Settle down, hija! My mother shakes her head and says, It's like I've always said. How many times have I said it? Those gypsies were never any good for her! Look! She's going crazy again!

· · ·

One cold evening I climb with difficulty but also determination up three flights of stairs. I asked Vicky to wait in her car with my crutches. Steadily, steadily I go up. Pull off the warm hat Amá knit for me. It's a little silly-looking but I don't want to hurt her feelings. She really tried. She used angora instead of the usual acrylic so at least it's soft and warm like a pink kitten on my head. Beneath the new wool coat I am wearing a gold lamé dress. We are coming from a party and after my third martini (martinis being only a television fifties cocktail to me until tonight) I am ready to confront my destiny.

The bulb on the second-floor landing is out, so I slide my feet across the floor and grope in the darkness like a blind lady until I touch the banister to the third floor. It's the last building on the block that hasn't been rehabbed and turned into a condo complex yet. I don't think anyone even lives on the second floor anymore. But there are people on the third floor because I can hear the muffled steps and voices. A young woman answers the door. She's dark, slight and looks like she's from India, but I know she's a calorra. Because she's gypsy, even though she's so small, she scares me a little. I know that's a prejudice, like those people who feel fear when they see a dark-skinned man coming toward them on the street. But gypsy women really do scare me. Maybe it's from the time Agustín's wife's curse almost killed me. This girl's got a lit cigarette in her hand and points with it to a closed bedroom door, He's in the room, she says casually in a strange accent.

I remember it's the same room that was his before, although I was only here once way back then. A man on the couch is snoring loudly. His hairy stomach bulges out of his shirt and a yellow striped cat lies on his chest. The place is more chaotic than I remember. Broken shades and double mismatched curtains to keep out the cold. There's a bulky old space heater taking up most of the living room. I place a sack of oranges on the table, next to a ristra of garlic and some big white and purple onions. The girl nods in acknowledgment and goes back to watching television with a boy who's about seven or eight perhaps. It's dark in the living room and their faces glow from the television light. They look like phantoms. I go to the bedroom slowly, slowly and push open the door. The room smells stale from too many cigarettes, an ashtray on a nightstand is filled with cigarette butts. He's asleep, fully clothed. A small lamp is on and so is a cassette player, playing something but so low I can't make it out. I won't remember the tune later although I tell myself to try. He wakes up and looks at me. His eyes are very red from being tired, hungover, high. Who knows? After a few seconds when he has focused, when it sinks in who it is standing above him, staring at him wide-eyed and speechless like he were Jesus or Satan, he smiles slowly. I can't imagine what my face looks like seeing him there in front of me after all this time, after so many roads we've each taken, we're like a pair of highway robbers who've bumped into each other by accident. If you meet the Buddha on the road, kill him, my yoga teacher told us once. The class stared at him at first like he was a psychopath, maybe with the same expression I have now, but then he explained. Unlike Christians, Buddhists don't think you should place too much power in another being or it will keep you from reaching your own truth.

The truth is his beautiful teeth are now caffeine-stained. Ah, Carmen . . . ! he says and starts to sit up, combs his tangled hair with his fingers, clears his throat. There's a bottle of liquor next to the bed and a glass. How've you been? he asks. I hear you're dancing again! he says and pours a drink and offers it to me. When I shake my head he drinks it down in one gulp. Not dancing, I say, singing.

Singing? Oh yeah! Right, right. Well, you have a good voice, you know that? he says. He pats the bed for me to sit down. I shake my head again. *I* . . . I start to say something, change my mind or lose the thought. I'm going. You were resting . . . And I turn around. ¡Oye! Carmen . . . ! he calls, but he does not get up and I do not stop.

·   ·   ·

*F*orty or not (but it is forty), I'm okay. I take a look in the mirror in the back of Amá's bedroom door. I may not dance professionally anymore but I still have a waist. Since I stopped dancing I got my breasts back too. It's the details that count. Although sometimes you have to look real close for the tiniest sign of something green. Like a lotus that has grown out of the mud underneath water and blossoms when it reaches light and a new life unfolds. I am a big lotus blossom, lovely and impermanent as everything else. In our own skin we can be reincarnated. You don't have to have a baby, reproduce yourself for a new and improved you. You don't have to die first. You don't have to die at all.

You just have to face the music pay the piper dance to the beat of your own drum and keep in mind that clichés aside all is fair in love and war.

So I'm ready.

chapter ten

Uno: Gold and blue-blue like
my aura . . .

Gold and blue-blue like my aura (or so I was told by Francis,
my new therapist who also does spiritual releasement or "getting rid
of your demons," as I call it) is the color scheme I came up with for
the new condo. Spiritual releasement is letting go through hypnosis
of all the many ways memories have worked themselves into your
joints and inhibit you or even stop you altogether from moving on.
Moving on is something I am doing at light-speed these days in my
weekly sessions with Francis, a licensed therapist with Oaxacan

throw rugs and soft piped-in music and a mobile above your head of paper angels. Just having a generally better disposition since my new recording-artist career has eased my aches and pains. I am still living with them but they are not stopping me anymore from living.

Vicky is more excited than I am about my condo, I think. We're almost roommates now, she says. Amá says, Don't worry too much about me, hija. I'm sure your father will keep coming up to check on me even when you're not here anymore. Besides, I have Macho. Remember that time he let you know I was having a heart attack? He'll bark if something happens . . . Maybe your father or your brother will hear from all the way downstairs.

Amá, if you want me to stay I will stay. I don't need to be on my own, I lie.

I'm not sure if I am way over my head with the purchase of a room of my own but if I am it will be worth it. I have my own bathroom. I don't have Macho sneaking onto my bed when I'm not around. I can play my stereo when I want. There are no television sets. Tell me, did I die and go to heaven, comadre? I ask Vicky my first night in my new home while we are eating pizza and having our own special housewarming for me.

Let's go out! she says. I'm too tired, I say. Come on, she says. Hey, let's go to the Olé Olé, huh? Wouldn't you like to rub that Courtney's nose in your fame just a little, comadre?

I think for a second. There's something about success that makes you become forgiving. Still, why not? What is success good for if you can't rub anyone's nose in it just a bit? I laugh. Then I laugh harder and can't stop when suddenly I realize I'm as incorrigible as everyone always said I was. Yeah, you *are* wicked! Vicky agrees, laughs hard with me and puts her arms around me so tight she knocks me down. We are nearly hysterical rolling on my new oak floor when she composes herself, helps me up, and says, And *that's* what I've always loved so much about you!

. . .

*T*he show at the Olé Olé gets started late. I have to fly to Long Beach next week, I whisper to Vicky, to start on the new CD. I really need to rest up as much as I can, not be out late like this, I say as I touch up my lipstick. All the way there I feel I've become the biggest diva I know (next to Vicky of course, in her cashmere outfit and Gucci tote bag), to the point that I can hardly stand myself anymore. But Vicky keeps saying, Just go with it, comadre! Enjoy what you've earned!

I'm a little nervous because I know that there's a chance that I'll run into Manolo tonight. There aren't too many places a gypsy like him can strut himself around in this town. I'm ready for him now, I think. But when I do finally spot him I still can't believe it is really him. He is at the bar swigging a fast espresso. He rubs his hands together and looks around. I know it is Manolo but I still find it hard to accept he is back. Chances are that he thought I was now rich and too famous for him. He was a man with a lot of calorro pride. He wouldn't come looking for me if he thought I would only kick him into the street like a begging dog.

Manolo is about to go on stage. The MC announces him over the mike. I put up my menu hoping he doesn't see me. I don't want him to see me yet. I want him to dance like he used to and I just want to watch and enjoy it. There's Manolo! Vicky says. I know that! I whisper. He's looking over here, did you know *that?* she asks. No, I say and put down the menu, trying to act casual and distracted but maybe I will come off looking a little lost instead, like he said I looked when he first saw me and fell in love with me. But I couldn't be further from lost now. No thanks to him.

Wait a minute, Vicky says. I wish she'd shut up, she's making me nervous. Is that . . . no . . . it can't be . . . ? Is that Agustín with him? Oh my God! It is! AGUSTÍN! my best friend calls out. Everyone looks around. A few customers recognize me. The MC looks over. Oh! she says. Is that Carmen la Coja! Lights, please! Let's give her a hand, everybody! Our wonderful singer from right here in Chicago . . . and wonderful dancer once, too! Carmen! Carmen, stand up for everybody to see you!

I will kill you, I say between clenched teeth to Vicky, who smiles and looks around at everybody as if they were applauding for her. No you won't, she says. Vicky grins and claps too and when Agustín comes up to us she puts out her arms. Oh Agustín, it's been so long, viejo!

Please don't call me "old man"! Agustín says. I feel old enough as it is with all these young people here! But you, Victoria, you look as beautiful as always, you never change! Tell me are you still at the bank . . . ?

No! ¡No, querido! Vicky says and still Agustín hasn't looked over at me. I am starting my own finance company. Whenever you need a loan please keep me in mind!

That's why Vicky is my best friend. She is more evil than I can dream of being although she seems to work a little harder at it. Agustín makes one last try to keep up with her digs but it is not going to work. He says, What? Querida, don't tell me you're *still* not married . . . ? What a shame!

No, Agustín . . . Victoria smiles and winks slyly at me while obviously enjoying pulling Agustín's leg. She takes a sip of wine. I'm saving myself for Carmen. *I* happen to think she's worth it, don't you? And my friend puts out a hand as if she were introducing us. Ah!, Agustín says and acknowledges me for the first time. His hair is a little thinner than I remember it, but surprisingly so is the rest of him. He is clean-shaven as always when acting the man about town. My old lifetime lover leans over and kisses me, not on the cheek but on the mouth. Funny how I had forgotten that, the way Agustín kissed and why I had kissed him for seventeen years. He whispered something in my ear over the music that was starting and I wasn't sure what it was but it sounded like, I'll see you later. I smiled and he smiled and Vicky smiled, all three of us aware of how many eyes were still on us, and then Agustín went up on stage to play for Manolo.

I think I ordered three shots of tequila during the show, but I could be wrong. Vicky said she wasn't counting, only that she was one up on me and it was time we went home. Watching Manolo dance after so many years, accompanied by Agustín's ferocious play-ing, shook me to my foundation. Manolo was dancing better than ever and Agustín's playing was more exquisite than I remembered too. What a pair! I sighed under my breath, because even if I hated each one a little, I loved them both for their talent as much as every moment I had spent with them alone and together, on stage and off. Then, just as I put down the glass for what was to be the last time that evening, Manolo took my hand.

I hadn't even noticed he had finished his performance. There were other dancers on stage and Agustín was still playing. Come with me, Manolo said. I got up and let him lead me to the back past the kitchen to an office. There were costumes and makeup everywhere. Street clothes on hangers or thrown on the floor. What is it? I asked Manolo, as if I had to ask when he closed the door behind him and searched my face as if in disbelief. Yeah, it's really me, I said sarcastically just before Manolo kissed me for the first time in five very long years.

Is it? he murmured, removing his vest, lifting my skirts. Manolo, is that you, I wondered but I wouldn't ask out loud and then, shaking a little, Manolío mío on his knees, I hear him whisper, Yes it *is* you . . . who else will it ever be . . . ?

Dos: You're like the dwarf who thought he was tall . . .

You're like the dwarf who thought he was tall because he spit far, I said to Agustín one night when he came over to my blue and gold condo with a view of the lake. Agustín laughed when I used that old gypsy expression on him to tease him. He came over with a bottle of Carlos Primero brandy just like the old days. So how's the wife and kids? I ask, getting two glasses out. But he takes me aback when he says, None for me. I don't drink anymore. Then he asks, What kids? Come on, Agustín, I say. Meanwhile I'm thinking, Tigers don't change their stripes. So what if he's a wonderful musician and was the man in most of my life. So what? Nine, Agustín. Did you forget you have nine children including a pair of twins? Come on, I say again. Courtney told me everything and that cantaor who was performing here with her a while ago said it too. Anyway, so do you want an espresso then? I head for the kitchen and he follows me. No, I don't drink coffee anymore, either. It's bad for my stomach.

What will you have then?

Diet Coke, if you have it, he says.

Diet Coke? Maybe the tiger sent his striped suit to the laundry, I think to myself. Before I figure out how to ask Agustín about his new taste in beverages, Agustín's puzzled face changes. Courtney? he says. I thought you knew better than that, guapa! He starts to laugh a little. Since when does a gitana like you believe what a woman who was so jealous of her tells her? As for that guy . . . he'd say anything for a free drink! I also wouldn't be too surprised if he had a little thing for Courtney! And I'm not exaggerating when I say a little thing! Still laughing, Agustín lights a cigarette.

Don't smoke in my house, I say, it's bad for my voice. He looks around, sees there are no ashtrays and goes to the sink to snuff it out. Oo-yoo-yoo! he says, like I'm putting on airs. When he throws it away, I ask, Now are you going to tell me that you don't have nine children? I pour the two glasses of Diet Coke, eyeing him all the while and before I take a sip I already know Courtney had me fooled but good. Agustín shakes his head. Not one. I don't even have a wife anymore, for that matter. She left me for a gajo. I don't blame her. I didn't even go after her. Guess what? Six months after she took off on me I heard she was pregnant! Do you think it was me all along?

No; as is your habit, your selective memory fails you, I say, but I don't really want to have this conversation. I guess I am happy for Inmaculada. I heard she was a good dancer!

Agustín laughs again. Ah! Carmen, I missed you so much for so long. You are one of a kind, but that Courtney really did pull your leg. My wife never danced. Even with two good feet she couldn't have competed with your dancing ever!

Why are you here? I ask Agustín, visibly annoyed. Besides the obvious, that is, I add. I can see how he looks at me, that same way he looked at me that night at the Olé Olé when he ran into Manolo and me coming out of the office, as if somewhere in his old-fashioned mind he thinks he has a claim on me, like an old worthless hat-check ticket. I had not seen him or Manolo since. In one night it was as if nothing had changed among the three of us. Agustín still did not want to give me up and Manolo was still torn.

There's no reason why we can't start again, Agustín says. You see what I mean? I ask. You really do think a lot of yourself, don't you, querido? The truth was I had surprised myself by feeling moved by Agustín at all the other night, but I wasn't about to admit it.

I think even more of you, he said. Thanks for the drink. He gave me another kiss on the mouth before he left. I don't know why I kissed him back.

I just felt like it.

.   .   .

After Manolo and I made love so hurriedly like a couple of safecrackers to get out of the back office of the Olé Olé quick, I did not wait for him to call me or look for me. He had not done it when he returned to Chicago, apparently some months before my brother Abel saw him on the street. He did not do it after I appeared like an aberration one night in the doorway of his bedroom. Yet we blended together as if it was the most natural thing to do when he led me by the hand past the Mexican cooks and Guatemalan busboys and the gringa-gaje waitresses to the little makeshift dressing room. We kissed and we held each other like two soldiers returning from the front, composed ourselves and went our separate ways again.

I wasn't waiting for him to show up at my door either like the

way Agustín did. It's absurd, I thought. Years have gone by. Alone I
have been through one hell after the next. And just as I am
climbing out, both Agustín and Manolo show up as if they had
only been gone a day, not even a day, just went out for a pack of
cigarettes and a drink, and both look at me upon their return as if
they can't understand why I am so surprised to see them. I'm
still mad at Agustín. I'm madder at Manolo. But the night
Agustín shows up a second time, uninvited as he is again, I let him
in.

What happened to your hand? I ask. His playing hand is completely bandaged. Never mind, he says. A little accident. He pulls
out his cigarettes and has a hard time getting one out. Don't smoke
in here, I say. Ah, it's just as well, he says, and throws the pack
aside. We talk about my new life as a singer, the concerts I've given
with Homero, my future plans, and then he looks around and says, I
don't blame you for hating me, Carmen.

I don't hate you, I say. I don't hate him, really. Maybe a little.
I'm hating him less with each kiss he steals from me, too. There are
a lot of do-you-remembers that make me laugh and smile and shake
my head because of how outrageous we were once and even the time
he insisted on spending the night to try to catch Manolo is a little
funny the way he tells it. Then Agustín says, You know what's really
funny . . . ? What? I ask. *This,* he says, lifting up his bandaged
hand. *This* is what's funny. I don't understand, I say. He still hasn't
told me about the accident. Your accident is funny? I ask. Ha!
Agustín says. Some accident!

He gets up, goes to pick up the pack of cigarettes, looks at me
and stops himself. Manolo has finally gotten his vengeance against
me, he says.

Manolo did that? I ask.

It was in a card game, Agustín says. He accused me of cheating and then he did this! Still Agustín doesn't say what it was exactly that happened to his hand, but I can guess now. Guess and say to myself, Enough is enough. You two aren't little boys or maybe you are! If you are going to try to kill each other over a card game, go back to wherever you two went off to before. Leave me alone. Both of you. I'll tell Manolo too . . . if I ever see him!

Calm down, calm down, Agustín says and takes hold of me. I love you as always and so does he. I challenged him to a card game the other night. I figured it was about time we see who is the better player. He accused me of cheating and just as I was about to pick up my winnings he pinned my hand down . . .

He did what? I ask.

Agustín smiles at me. Well, I think it's pretty obvious. But why are *you* so worked up? It's not like *you* are the one who's been put out of commission. Who knows when I'll be able to play guitar again or if I ever will! I don't dance much anymore, maybe I'll have to take singing lessons from *you* . . . !

I'm unnerved by the fact that Manolo is really a gambling, gold-tooth thug. Of course I always knew it but I never let myself believe it. When I'm able to say it, I am not just saying it, I'm going around the house ranting, ¡Ay madre mía! How is it possible that I spent so many years missing a good-for-nothing criminal! Okay, so maybe he's a great dancer and a great lover too, sorry Agustín, but still, just look! There's the proof! I point to Agustín's hand, pour myself a brandy, gulp it down, wipe my lips and go on ranting like that, half talking to myself, half to Agustín. Calm down, calm down, he says finally. He is amazingly calm himself for a man who has just lost his ability to make a living (at least legitimately) for the time being. And now what? I ask Agustín. Are you going to seek vengeance on Manolo for what he did to your hand?

Agustín laughed. Why should I? He laughed again. After all, I *did* cheat!

Tres: Not just one long-stemmed rose . . .

Not just one long-stemmed rose but thirty. That's how many Manolo brought me one evening. Five times half a dozen for each year we were apart, he said.

Come in, I said. I flung the huge bouquet on the couch and went back to the kitchen.

He had caught me in the middle of peeling fresh shrimp for dinner, in an apron and with my hair piled up on the top of my head. Worst of all, I wasn't wearing lipstick. No one ever saw me without my red lipstick, not even Vicky, whom I was cooking dinner for that evening. I want you to meet my new girlfriend, she'd said to me a few days earlier. This one could be *the* one! Ever since I had moved into Vicky's building, I realized that despite her commitments to her job and to her brother, Virgil, she still had time to fool around. Every time I ran into her in the hallway she had a date coming in or going out of her apartment. What's up with you? I asked. What do you mean? she said. Being a professional woman in a world filled with Puritanical ideas about love, she kept her gay life pretty private. Well, then it's time to bring her home to meet your "family," I said to my comadre. I was making shrimp fricassee for starters when the doorbell rang.

I had never made shrimp fricassee. But one night when I was reading the account of the Conquest of Mexico by Friar Sahagún he described an Aztec dish which came down to a shrimp fricassee. You use a lot of *P* ingredients, pumpkin seeds, pimientos, chile piquín, and of course, *peeled* jumbo shrimp. So there I was peeling shrimp when the love of my life returned.

There was a lot more to the Conquest of Mexico, as I was learning, than extracting Indian recipes. It was a story of love and betrayal, like all those paperback romances sold in grocery stores promise. A story of two great men, one lived and one died. And one very great although misunderstood woman. High drama. I couldn't take it. I'd pick up my fat library edition at bedtime, read a few pages, cry myself to sleep, then pick it up again the next night. My copy was overdue.

How did you find my new place? I asked Manolo as I went back to my Aztec shrimp fricassee. Your mother told me, Manolo said. He was wearing a midnight-blue silk shirt under his dress jacket. When he gave me a little kiss on the mouth I took a good whiff. He smelled really good, a little like anise. It wasn't cologne or aftershave. It was Manolo.

My mother? I asked. Why would she give my address to you? She doesn't even know you!

Well, she does now, Manolo laughed. I told her I am going to be her son-in-law and she said, Here, this is where she lives.

Manolo, I said, you are so full of it. The one who gave you my address was probably my good-for-nothing brother Abel. With a bribe that guy would sell out his own grandma!

No, Manolo insisted, it was my future mother-in-law. And she said to tell you, Don't forget to come over Saturday morning to make the tortillas for your father!

Yeah, it was my mother all right. I thought about mentioning that Agustín had come over with his bandaged hand but changed my mind. That was between them. Don't you want to put your roses in water? Manolo asked. He looked a little hurt by my rejection of his gift. But all the roses in the world were not going to make up for five lost years. You do it, I said. The vases are in the cabinet. Manolo went about gathering up the flowers, which had fallen heavily like a corpse on the couch, and put them all in vases, sucking a finger each time a thorn stuck. Meanwhile I sang softly at my stove. Manolo and I did not say much to each other until he finished. You did a nice job arranging them, I said indifferently, looking around where he had placed the vases. He smiled. Then he took my hand just as I was about to make a puree in the blender—the modern equivalent of the molcajete the Aztecs used to grind. Self-consciously I brought the other one up to my nose. Just as I thought, it smelled a little fishy. I pulled the clip out of my hair and let it fall down over my shoulders. Somehow, I just didn't picture this reunion with Manolo with me looking like a fishmarket woman. But he didn't seem to notice. Manolo swallowed hard, then he spoke. Carmen, I didn't come sooner because I was ashamed.

Yes, I said, You chose your friend over me.

No, Manolo said, I chose my godfather . . . because I had to, because my father had asked it of me before he died, because of our ways, many reasons that you don't accept. I understand. You're not one of us. That hurt me. But I shouldn't have let you love me if I believed we shouldn't be together.

So, I said, pulling my fishy hand away, why did you come here tonight?

Manolo paced around for a minute. Carmen, you became my life. You've always known that. And you will always be my life. When you decide that I am your life too, let me know. I have a performance tonight, come by later, if you'd like. Otherwise, you will know how to find me.

And if I don't look for you again, Manolo? I asked. If expecting you to come back for so long, just the way you did tonight, your arms loaded down with roses for me and you . . . Well, what could I say about Manolo that my eyes weren't telling him? What if all that waiting took away every last ounce of desire to so much as pick up the telephone now to call you?

Manolo nodded. He reached for the worn-out wallet in his back pocket to show me something he was carrying. It was a yellowed newspaper clipping preserved in plastic, a picture of us together. MANOLÍO AND CARMEN LA COJA, it read, PERFORMING SATURDAY NIGHT. He showed it to me and took it back. It's my good-luck piece, he said, putting it away again.

Cuatro: Where there's pleasure a scab doesn't itch . . .

Where there's pleasure, a scab doesn't itch, Agustín said to me one night when we had become lovers again, perforated hand and all. It's another one of his old Rom sayings. Sarapia sat pesquital ne punzava, is what he actually said.

So are you the scab or am I? I asked. I looked at his hand with the stitches on front and back in the shape of a cross and shook my head. Manolo! I thought. Manolo! Agustín sighed. ¡Ah! That kid! And then we fell asleep.

As if sleeping with Agustín again in this lifetime, sleeping and more were not peculiar enough reoccurrences, an odd déjà vu and life playing a little at vengeance with me, then there was the fact that I was no longer obsessing over Manolo. I had waited for him to show up for five years and for five years thought of nothing but being with him again. But since we made love in the back office it had all stopped. My heart was at peace because Manolo had proven that he had never stopped loving me.

But there remain things that Manolo has not worked out. He still belongs to the night. He still belongs to faraway Grimm fairy-tale countries, to customs I'm not convinced are of use to any woman anymore, calorra or not. So the day I do see Manolo, mi manchorro, again, when he comes back another night and takes me by the shoulders and says, Please Carmen give me a chance, all I can say to him is another one of Agustín's expressions: A dog and a wolf don't make a good household.

A dog and a wolf nothing! Vicky scoffs. Try three wolves, Carmen girl!

Settle down, hija! my amá says when I tell her about my dilemma. Choose one or neither but settle down with someone! It's not too late to have a child if you want!

A corn that's picked while still green has no taste, I say. That's how I feel about Manolo. But sometimes when Manolo calls I say, Okay, you can come see me. He has resumed his cooking experiments too (with too much garlic). But he measures out his love just right.

Sure, come over! I also say to Agustín on other nights when

he calls, since he has learned to call or else he stays outside where no one buzzes him up. And when I don't want to see anyone I don't answer the telephone at all, pull the shades down tight, put on my own CD on the new stereo with six speakers around the apartment and just dance. I dance and dance and dance.

ALSO BY ANA CASTILLO

THE MIXQUIAHUALA LETTERS

This epistolary novel in the tradition of Julio Cortazar's *Hopscotch* is the noted poet's first. It focuses on the friendship between two strong and fiercely independent Hispanic women and examines Mexican and Hispanic forms of love and gender conflict and the role that female friendships play within it.

Fiction/Literature/0-385-42013-7

SAPOGONIA

In her second novel, Castillo examines the obsessive struggle between a man and a woman, two natives of the metaphorical country of Sapogonia. In the battle for control over each other, the author subtly defines the struggle of all mestizos —the conflict of a mixed heritage of conquistador and conquered—which can never be resolved.

Fiction/Literature/0-385-47080 0

ANCHOR BOOKS
Available at your local bookstore, or call toll-free to order:
1-800-793-2665 (credit cards only).